P9-BJB-503

I Was a
Fifth-Grade Zebra

I Was a Fifth-Grade Zebra

Nancy J. Hopper

Dial Books for Young Readers
New York

Published by Dial Books for Young Readers
A Division of Penguin Books USA Inc.
375 Hudson Street
New York, New York 10014

Design by Julie Rauer
First Edition
1 3 5 7 9 10 8 6 4 2

Library of Congress Cataloging in Publication Data
Hopper, Nancy J.
I was a fifth-grade zebra / by Nancy J. Hopper.
p. cm.
Summary: When other girls in her fifth-grade class seem to be
obsessed with boys, Chelsea Zeller tries to imitate her role
model, Dian Fossey, as she examines her identity
and her own feelings about boys.
ISBN 0-8037-1420-3 (tr); ISBN 0-8037-1595-1 (lib. bdg.)
[1. Schools—Fiction. 2. Interpersonal relations—Fiction.] I. Title.
PZ7.H7792Zaad 1993 [Fic]—dc20 92-30731 CIP AC

To my parents,
Joyce B. and David L. Swartz

I Was a
Fifth-Grade Zebra

One

~~~~~

The day Rachel placed her invitation on my desk, snow still glistened along the top bar of the swing set and on the curve of the slide outside our classroom windows. But suddenly, Room 14 felt as hot as summer—to me, anyway.

PARTY! PARTY! was printed in letters like candles across the front of the card. On the cake beneath the candles was written, AND YOU'RE INVITED! Inside the invitation was Rachel's name, a time, a date, and her address. The bad part was written in cursive underneath: *Wear your best party dress and bring a boy.*

"My best party dress is a pair of jeans," I said.

Danielle Rogers, who sat catty-corner to me, sighed and rolled her eyes to the ceiling.

"You wore a dress on our Scout trip to the ballet," Rachel pointed out.

"That was last year. I don't even have that dress anymore. Besides, I can't . . ."

Danielle lowered her gaze from the ceiling to stare at me. Her blue eyes protruded slightly and weren't very friendly.

"Can't what?" asked Rachel.

"Ask a boy!"

"Of course you can."

"But, Rachel, I don't want to!"

"Then you'll just have to miss all the fun," said Danielle.

"I don't know anybody to ask," I told Rachel, trying to ignore Danielle. If Rachel wanted boys at her party, why didn't *she* invite them?

"Come on, Chelsea," said Rachel. "Everybody knows you like C.R."

The very second Rachel said that, Mr. Feeny entered the room. Some of the other kids stopped talking, so the end of Rachel's sentence came out into near silence. She might as well have announced it over the public-address system.

"I do not!" I said.

"You practically drool every time he walks by on the playground," said Danielle.

"That's not true," I protested. "I practically *hate*

C. R. He smells like cat dirt, and I wouldn't invite him if he were the last person on earth."

"Chelsea and Danielle," interrupted Mr. Feeny. "Please keep your conversation until after dismissal. Rachel, I don't believe you belong on that side of the room."

As Rachel returned to her seat, Danielle gave me a disgusted look. "What an *infant*," she said.

That was when Gina Morelli, my best friend, came into the room. She hung the pass to the girls' lavatory on its hook over the wastebasket, crossed to her desk, beside mine, and slid into her seat. As she opened the lid of her desk, her long hair swept forward to hide her face from me.

I slumped, wishing I could make myself invisible. While I was slumping, I sneaked a look at C. R. Halloway, who sat behind Rachel.

C. R. was trying to act as if he hadn't heard a thing, but he didn't fool me. Beneath his short hair his squarish face was unusually serious. His shoulders were hunched, and he was listening to the teacher as if Mr. Feeny were giving out the winning number in this week's lottery.

"Three people still have not come up with acceptable subjects for their VIP reports," Mr. Feeny told us in his rumbly voice. "Who can remind them of the guidelines for choosing a Very Important Person to write about?"

A lot of kids raised their hands, but I was not among them.

"Kendra?" asked Mr. Feeny.

"The VIP has to be a man or woman who has made a lasting contribution to the Earth or its inhabitants."

"Very good." Mr. Feeny stroked his mustache. He is tall and thin with short gray-brown hair. Usually he wears brown suits to school, but that day he was wearing a navy sweater with a pale blue shirt and a striped tie. "Lindsey?"

"A person who changed things for the better," Lindsey said. Her voice always sounds squeaky, as if it needs to be oiled.

"Joe Montana did that!" said Chad. "I don't see why you won't let me do my report on him."

"Jerome, tell Chad why Joe Montana is not a good choice for this assignment."

I didn't listen to Jerome's answer. I'd known from the very first day the report was assigned that I wanted to write on Dian Fossey, who studied mountain gorillas in deepest Africa. I'd already begun reading about her—and besides, I had other problems. I really hate to hurt people's feelings, and I hadn't been very flattering to C.R.

After dismissal Rachel, Danielle, and some of the other girls gathered at the front of the room. As I passed them on my way to the door, Rachel said, "I don't see why you're making such a big deal about inviting a boy to my party, Chelsea." Sounding like Danielle, she added, "Sometimes I think you don't even like me anymore."

"I do like you," I told her, "but I wish you weren't so boy crazy."

"I'm *not* boy crazy," Rachel protested.

"Talking about boys all the time is boring," I pointed out. "And the way you hang around them and flirt means you're boy crazy." I glanced at the other girls, thinking one of them would back me up.

Lindsey looked away. Jill Ebert frowned, and Gina seemed a bit embarrassed.

"You are so immature," said Danielle, who thinks she knows everything because her mother works at the mental health center. "In reality, you're socially retarded."

"No way!" Although I wasn't sure what "socially retarded" meant, I figured it was no compliment. "I just happen to think it's a dumb idea to ruin a perfectly good party with a bunch of boys."

"Boys won't ruin the party," said Jill.

"They will too," I said, even though I didn't really believe it was true. I stuck my chin out. "If I had a party, I wouldn't make the other girls ask boys."

"Well, it's *my* party," said Rachel, "and if you want to get past the front door, you'd better not show up without one."

"Right." Danielle tossed her long sandy-colored curls back over her shoulders. Her lips curved upward in triumph. "Stay home if you want to be a baby all your life. It's not as if we'll miss you. You wouldn't fit in anyway."

TWO

~~~~~

Am I socially retarded?"
I asked Gina on the way out of the building.

"Unh-unh." She shook her head.

"At least I'm not stuck on myself like Danielle . . ." I let the words trail off, wanting Gina to say she liked me exactly the way I am, but she didn't get the hint.

"I think it was mean of Danielle to say that," I added as we walked down the long sidewalk from the school, "just because I'm embarrassed to ask a boy to go to the party."

"I am too," Gina admitted, her greenish eyes looking worried behind her glasses. "I have an upset stomach just thinking about it."

"See!" My mood lightened. "I'm no different from any other girl!"

Gina got an odd expression on her face, as if she didn't believe me.

"Name one way," I challenged. "Just one way I'm different."

"What about Scamper?"

"Scamper was a gift!" I protested. He was my pet tarantula that Juliet had given me for my eleventh birthday. I'd called him Scamper because he could run so fast.

"It was still a mistake to bring a giant spider to school for the pet parade."

"I had to bring *something*," I muttered, thinking that it was insensitive of Gina to bring up Scamper because it had only been a few weeks since he'd died. Scamper might have been a spider—a short-lived one—but he was a very nice spider. "Scamper doesn't really count. He's not even around any more."

"You write poems," said Gina. Then she added hastily, "Good poems."

Ignoring the compliment, I said, "Everybody has a hobby. You play the piano."

"Me and about fifty other kids at school. The only difference is that I play better than they do."

"A lot better." Gina was so good at the piano, she'd been invited to play with the Cleveland Youth Orchestra.

I said good-bye at her corner and trudged on home,

still brooding over Danielle's telling me I wouldn't fit in at the party. Maybe Gina was right, I decided. Even if writing poems wasn't weird, it probably was a mistake to show them to other kids. Jerome had teased me for weeks about the one about squishing mud between my toes.

Once I'd have charged into the house and dumped all of my troubles on Mom. The problem was that I'd begun to feel as if Mom didn't really understand when something went wrong in my life. I mean, she tried and all that. But most of the time she ended up lecturing on how I could fix it, when what I wanted was loads of sympathy and maybe a few dozen chocolate-chip cookies.

I peeled off my coat as I entered the house and hung it in the closet. Then I headed for the kitchen, where I knew Mom would be waiting to hear about my day.

Mom was perched on a high stool at the lunch bar that we have instead of a kitchen table. She must have stopped at the bakery on the way home from work because there was a plate of brownies and a cup of coffee in front of her. A glass of milk and an empty plate were on the opposite side of the counter.

At the sight of the brownies, my spirits rose. I

climbed onto the stool nearest the empty plate and reached for a brownie. "Where's Juliet?" I asked.

"She went to the mall with Marty."

"Oh." I took a huge bite of brownie. It was thick and fudgy, just the way I like them. I washed that bite down with milk, then took another, smaller bite. Danielle's criticism and the thought of the party had ruined my appetite. I put the brownie on the plate.

"Is there something wrong?" asked Mom.

"No." I shook my head and drank more milk, trying to throw Mom off the track. "I'm just not hungry."

"What did you do in school?"

"Learned about the skeletal system." I eyed Mom over the rim of my glass. People say we look a lot alike, with our narrow faces and straight dark brown hair. We both have slightly tilted blue-gray eyes too, and an interest in biology—which is no surprise since Mom is a nurse.

"Did you ever wish you were still a little kid and didn't have to think about some things?" I asked her.

"What kind of things?"

"Boy-girl things." I pulled the crumpled party invitation from my pocket. "Like this."

Mom smoothed the invitation flat to read it. "This doesn't seem exactly life shattering," she observed.

I made a face.

"Besides, Rachel's a friend of yours. I'd think you'd want to go to her party."

"I just don't see why we're supposed to invite boys. I *hate* boys," I said, "and I'm not going to ask one to a party."

"You'll miss all the fun."

"So what?" I shrugged, then hunched over my plate, avoiding Mom's eyes. The memory of Danielle's triumphant smile and how she'd told me I wouldn't fit in blanked out the first part of Mom's next sentence. I caught the end of it.

". . . single boy in your class who isn't overwhelmingly repulsive?"

"C.R. Halloway's okay, and I think he used to like me . . ."

"Used to?" My sister, Juliet, had arrived home and came into the kitchen in time to hear Mom's question. She reached between us for a brownie, then leaned her elbows on the end of the counter and watched me while she ate it.

"Until this afternoon, when Danielle was telling the whole class how weird I act when C.R.'s around.

I got mad and yelled that I hate C.R." I gulped milk. It was warm, as if it had been out of the refrigerator too long. "So now C.R.'s mad at me," I finished.

"Did you apologize?" Mom asked.

"For what?"

"For hurting his feelings."

"Of course not! I was too embarrassed."

Mom tilted her head and looked at me sternly. "It's a good idea to keep your mouth shut if you can't say something nice," she said.

"Tell me about it," I muttered.

"You brought this on yourself, Chelsea," she added. Another minute and she'd be lecturing me about how people should be civilized to each other.

"I must have missed something," said Juliet, looking from me to Mom and back again. "Why do you have to locate a boy who isn't overwhelmingly repulsive?"

"To invite him to Rachel's birthday party," I told her. "The problem is that I don't want to invite a boy."

"What *do* you want?" asked Juliet.

"To be like the other girls!" I wailed. "But all they want to talk about is boys and dating and all that yucky stuff!"

Juliet raised her eyebrows so far, they disappeared under her fringe of curls. Her hair is normally straight and brown like mine, but she tortures it with permanents and rinses until it's a fuzzy blond. "You're no different from any other girl in the fifth grade," she said.

"I am too. I'm practically a freak."

"Says who?"

"Danielle, for example."

"You're not a freak," Juliet told me. "Everybody is nervous when they first become aware of the opposite sex."

"Not you," I accused.

" 'Fraid so." She nodded, one corner of her mouth lifting higher than the other in its lopsided smile. "Mom practically had to force me out of the house on my first date."

Mom and Juliet exchanged glances, both of them smiling as if they shared some kind of special secret. Then Mom looked at me. "Sometimes baby birds need a little nudge out of the nest," she told me.

"What if they can't fly?" I demanded.

"Oh, Chelsea. Stop being so dramatic!"

I made a protesting noise deep in my throat.

"I want you to apologize to C.R. tomorrow morning," she added.

"Then you can invite him to the party," said Juliet.

"What if he won't go?"

"Ask another boy."

"And another," said Mom, "until one of them accepts."

"Uh . . . ah," I mumbled, feeling cornered. Then I said, "But I don't have a party dress, and I don't know how to walk in high heels or act at this kind of party, or how to talk to a boy."

"It's not *that* bad." Mom reached across the counter to put a hand on my arm. "You've been talking to boys practically all your life. We'll find you a perfectly beautiful dress, and help you to learn about the rest."

I hesitated, thinking. Shopping for a party dress might be fun, and maybe I could get Mom into the pet store, where I could buy a replacement for Scamper.

"Chelsea?" said Mom.

"All right," I agreed reluctantly.

"Promise?" asked Juliet.

"I promise," I said. With a wild surge of optimism, I made a promise to myself too. I would invite a boy, get all dressed up, go to the party, and pretend to have a wonderful time. I would act normal if it killed me.

Three

~~~~~~

Except for my VIP report, I didn't have any homework that evening, which was lucky. All I seemed able to think of was the promise I'd made to Mom and Juliet. Even when I was reading about Dian Fossey, my brain kept coming back to two big B's—Being different and Boys.

I read that Dian Fossey had named the camp she founded Karisoke, after the Karisimbi and Visoke Mountains in Africa, where it was located. The people who lived near the camp had their own traditions. Since some of these traditions were very harmful to the mountain gorillas, Dian didn't get along very well with many of the local people.

Just like Danielle and Rachel with me, I decided. They had a tradition of chasing boys and I didn't. Mom and Juliet had different traditions than I did too. After all, Mom had married my father, and Juliet always seemed to have a boyfriend.

I put my VIP report aside and spent the rest of the evening and part of the night trying to come up with a way to wiggle out of my promise. I spent so much time thinking about it that by morning my brain ached.

"While I couldn't sleep last night I had an idea," I told Gina when I met her at the corner.

"Just one?" she teased.

"You can come over to my house the night of Rachel's party, maybe for dinner. We can rent a couple of videos and make popcorn. I bet Mom'd let you sleep over."

"What about the party?"

"Who wants to go to a stupid party with boys?"

"I do," said Gina. When we'd merged with the crowd of other kids entering the building, she added, "Your hair looks nice."

"Juliet styled it this morning." My sister had made a long French braid for me, starting at the top of my head and gathering in new hair as she braided. When she'd finished, Juliet leaned forward, gave me a quick kiss on the cheek, and whispered, "Don't forget your promise."

Apologize to C.R. That had been easy to promise, but it sure wasn't easy to do. He didn't show up for school until the late bell was sounding. At lunch we sat at different tables, and recess was canceled because of rain.

Besides, just the idea of acting sweet and gooey toward a boy made me feel as if I'd eaten a large bag of marshmallows. As for my being like the other girls—Juliet didn't know what she was talking about. While Mr. Feeny explained the respiratory system during the last class of the day, I secretly eyed the girls in Room 14.

Gina had long reddish-gold hair and green eyes. Rachel was chubby, but she had eyes the color of a melted Hershey's bar and naturally curly black hair. She also had a figure, even though she was younger than most of the other girls. Kendra was pretty and popular, Jill—so little and cute her picture could be on a valentine. Even Danielle, who was a scratch-cat, could be all purrs when she wanted something.

And what is Chelsea like, I thought, trying to be honest with myself.

Physically, I rated just okay. Well, maybe a little better than okay. My hair was very shiny right after I washed it, and the bump on the bridge of my nose was barely noticeable. My eyes were kind of nice. I had a skinny body and long legs. Unlike Lindsey, I wasn't particularly shy. Gina thought I was popular, but I wasn't so sure. After all, Danielle didn't like me.

C.R. probably didn't like me anymore either. I groaned inside. How was I ever going to get up the courage to invite him to the party?

Mr. Feeny drew a diagram on the chalkboard. The lumpy object in the middle was supposed to be a lung, but it looked like a cloud to me. I took a deep breath to check out my respiratory system. It was still working.

Behind me Kendra whispered, "Did you invite anyone to the party yet?"

I shook my head.

"Neither did I."

Since Kendra is African American, I figured she'd probably ask either Dominik or Jerome, the only other black kids in Room 14. Or she could invite Anthony Everette, who is in Mrs. Rudolph's room. Anthony's a really neat kid.

The day dragged on. At last Mr. Feeny told us to clear our desks and get our coats for dismissal. I gritted my teeth. Maybe I could take a shortcut and just ask C.R. to the party. That would be practically the same as apologizing.

On the way out of the room, I pushed between Jerome and C.R. In the process, I thumped Jerome in the stomach with an elbow.

"Watch it," said Jerome. "That's sweet meat."

"Sorry," I said quickly, then wondered why it was so easy to apologize to Jerome and so hard to apologize to C.R.

I followed C.R., my eyes fixed on the back of his orange shirt. Maybe he didn't care that I'd said those ugly things about him. Maybe he still liked me, at least a little bit. I caught up with him near our lockers.

"C.R.," I said.

C.R.'s eyes are large and the same light blue as the sky on a clear day.

At least he didn't look mad at me. I licked my lips. "Will you go to Rachel's party with me?" I asked.

"No," said C.R. He looked steadily at me, as if he'd never seen me before.

"No?" I echoed.

"NO," C.R. repeated loudly.

Danielle, who was standing nearby, snickered.

I could feel my face getting hot, but I didn't give

up. "Listen, C. R.," I said. "I didn't mean . . . I . . .
I—"

"*Love you,*" finished Jerome. "Chelsea loves C. R.!"
He grabbed my braid and tugged.

"Jerome!" I wheeled on him. Jerome's round
brown face had an enormous grin. His dark eyes
danced with mischief. He made kissing sounds at
me, then chanted, "Chelsea and C. R., sitting in a
tree, k-i-s-s-i-n-g."

"Cut it out!" I yelled.

"Whoo-ee!" Jerome threw his hands in the air.
"You are scary!" He jive-walked backward down the
hall.

So I wouldn't have to see the expression on C. R.'s
face, I turned to my locker, took my book bag out,
filled it, and slung it on my back.

"Chelsea," said Jerome, singing it. "Chel-sea."

Like a fool, I looked at him.

Jerome stuck out his stomach, put one hand on his
hip, and wiggled his butt. "Oh, C. R.," he cooed. "I
love the smell of cat dirt."

Rachel, whose locker is near mine, giggled.

"Kissy, kissy," said Jerome. He made a noise with
his lips.

That did it. I charged him.

Jerome ran down the hall toward the media center. I ran after him, my book bag thumping against my back, my heels clattering on the floor.

Jerome was fast, but I was faster. I caught one sleeve of his jacket, but the smooth, satiny material slipped from my fingers.

He dodged around a group of kindergartners and tried to take cover between the water fountain and the open door of the media center. He wedged himself into the small space on the floor, his knees pulled tight to his chest, his arms wrapped around them.

"You keep your mouth shut or you'll be sorry," I threatened.

"Help! Somebody save me!" Jerome shouted. Then he laughed.

"Hit him!" yelled a boy in the crowd that was forming.

"Fight!" yelled somebody else. "Fight!"

Jerome's eyes gleamed with delight. "Kissy, kissy," he said.

"Jerome's going to get beat up by a girl," yelled Dominik, sounding mightily pleased by the prospect.

"Chelsea loves C.R.," a girl chanted behind me. I didn't know who.

". . . sitting in a tree," came from another direction.

"K-i-s-" began Jerome.

"SHUT UP!" I leaned over and shouted right into his face. I made a fist and brought it up, ready to punch him.

"Chelsea, stop it," ordered a new voice. "Stand up, Jerome. I'm surprised at both of you."

The principal was glaring at me, her face not ten inches from mine.

Somebody whistled. I straightened, suddenly aware that the hall was packed with kids.

"You two come with me," Mrs. Mumford told us. "There is no excuse for this type of behavior."

"Oh, C.R.," someone called sweetly from the back of the crowd. "I love you!"

Four

~~~~~~~~

I was hot, sweaty, and totally humiliated as I followed the principal. I only hoped Jerome was suffering as much as I was. We entered the outer office, went past the secretary's desk, and continued on into Mrs. Mumford's private office.

"Sit," she told us. Then she went to speak to her secretary.

I stared at my hands, wondering what Mom was going to do when she found out I'd been fighting. A hard lump formed in my throat. I tried to swallow it but couldn't.

"All right." Mrs. Mumford came back into her office, leaving the door open. She went to stand behind her desk. "I want to know exactly what was going on with you two."

I couldn't think of anything that would sound good, so I kept silent.

"Look at me, Chelsea," said Mrs. Mumford.

For a second my eyes seemed frozen in their sockets, but then I managed to raise them slowly from my hands to the front of the blue desk, then up across the pen set and the dark blue blotter covered with papers, to the principal.

Like Mr. Feeny, Mrs. Mumford is new in Oakway Elementary this year. She isn't very tall, and she's skinny too, but it didn't take her long last fall to get a reputation for being strict, especially about fighting.

I dug a thumbnail into the palm of my hand, hoping I wouldn't have any pain, that I was having a nightmare.

My nail hurt my hand all right.

"What happened?"

Although I hadn't seen any lightning, thunder rumbled in the distance. Rain lashed against the only window in the principal's office. Beyond it, everything looked gray.

"Jerome was teasing me and I was trying to make him stop," I said in a low voice.

"Jerome?" Mrs. Mumford looked at him.

Before Jerome could answer, a kid burst into the outer office. "There's a fight on the playground!" he

27

shrieked. "They're rolling in the mud and biting and everything!"

The secretary jumped to her feet.

Mrs. Mumford was around her desk in a flash. "Stay here," she ordered over her shoulder as she rushed out of the office.

She couldn't have been gone more than a few minutes, but it seemed like an hour. I watched rain beat on the window and tried not to think. Once I glanced across the room at Jerome, whose chair was closer to the door.

Jerome's elbows were on his knees, his chin propped in his hands. He was staring intently at the floor.

I wanted to yell at him, tell him it was all his fault we were in trouble, but I didn't. Nobody told me to chase Jerome down the hall, to corner him by the water fountain.

If Mom found out I did that, she'd tell me I should have ignored his teasing or acted as if I didn't care. She always says, "Sticks and stones may break my bones, but words will never hurt me."

Mrs. Mumford returned, looking ten times more angry—and more interesting—than when she'd left. She was dragging one mud-spattered boy, and Mr.

Harris, our maintenance man, was dragging another. "Sit here," said Mrs. Mumford as she deposited her captive on an orange plastic chair next to the Lost and Found box. "Mr. Harris, will you keep an eye on these two for a few minutes?"

"Sure thing." Mr. Harris folded his arms across his chest.

The principal shut the door to her office, the kind of shutting my mother calls a slam, but not when she does it. The right sleeve of her pale-gray suit was torn at the shoulder seam, and there were big splashes of muddy water on her skirt and legs. Her shoes went *squelch, squelch* as she crossed the room to her closet. She took a towel from the closet and wiped her face. Then she peeled off her suit jacket and put it on a hanger. Her silky pink blouse was a little wet, but there was only one spot of mud on it.

"Where were we?" She rubbed at her hair with the towel.

"Jerome was teasing me and I was trying to make him stop," I told her.

"Oh. Right." Mrs. Mumford hung up the towel, then went to her filing cabinets where she opened a drawer and pulled out a file. She glanced at it, put it back, and then did the same thing with another file.

When she went to stand behind her desk, most of the mess on her skirt was hidden from view. "Jerome? What do you have to say?"

"Nothing."

"Surely you have something."

"No, Ma'am."

The principal glanced from Jerome to me and back again.

Jerome cleared his throat. Then he said, "It was all my fault. Chelsea didn't do anything wrong."

"Chelsea?"

I wanted to tell her the fight really *was* Jerome's fault, but that wouldn't be completely true. Besides, Jerome was already willing to take all the blame. "I shouldn't have chased him," I admitted.

"There is no record of either one of you having been in this office for disciplinary reasons," said Mrs. Mumford, "and I certainly am sorry to see you here now, in your very last year in this building."

My stomach lurched and I swallowed nervously.

In the outer office Mr. Harris told one of the boys to sit down and shut up.

"All right," Mrs. Mumford said at last. "Since both of you are aware of your responsibility, I'm going to let you off with a warning. But I never, and I do mean *never,* want to see you in here again."

"Okay," I whispered.

"Yes, Ma'am," said Jerome.

"Thanks, Jerome," I said as we cleared the door of the outer office. "You were awesome."

"I know."

My stomach felt better, and even the weather had improved. The downpour had slowed to a steady rain, and the only thunder sounded far away. We stopped under the overhang at the front of the building, watching the rain. There wasn't another kid in sight.

"I missed the bus," said Jerome. "My mother's going to kill me."

I looked at him. Despite the fact he's shorter than I am and a little bit fat, Jerome's not bad looking. He's popular too, and has a great sense of humor—when it's not directed at me.

"Hey, Jerome," I said. "You know about Rachel's party?"

"Yeah." He peered toward the street as if hoping a big yellow bus would materialize out of nothing. Then he pulled up his jacket collar and set off into the rain.

I fell into step beside him. "You want to go?"

"No, thanks. Girls' parties are dumb."

"There'll be tons of food."

"There will?"

"Sure," I promised recklessly. "Potato chips and sandwiches, birthday cake, ice cream. Loads of stuff like that."

"Would I have to buy a present?"

"Since I asked you, I'd get the present."

When Jerome hesitated, I added, "Rachel's parents have lots of video games, and her mom's a super cook."

"I'll go." Jerome put out a hand, palm up.

I smacked my palm on his, making a crisp slap. "It's a deal," I told him, wondering why I didn't invite Jerome in the first place. I'd have a lot more fun with him than with C.R., who might have wanted to hold hands or get mushy. "Want to stop at my house? My mom will drive you home."

"Okay." For someone who'd just been invited to a party, Jerome didn't sound very excited. He muttered, "My mother will probably take away my TV privileges for a week and ground me besides."

"Blame the whole thing on me."

"That won't make any difference." Jerome came to an abrupt halt as a long cream-colored car passed us, then put two fingers in his mouth and whistled.

The car pulled to the curb like a taxi. At the wheel was Kendra's mother, Mrs. Reed, who teaches first grade in our school. Kendra rolled down a window.

"Want a ride?" she asked.

"Sure do!" Jerome ran to the car, pulled a back door open, and dove inside.

"Chelsea?"

"No thanks," I told her. "I only live a few blocks from here, and I'm already wet."

"See you tomorrow," Kendra said as she rolled up the window.

"Bye!" yelled Jerome.

I'd snagged a boy for the party! "Hooooray!" I shouted, then put my feet together and jumped into the center of a puddle.

Water splashed high around me, flowing back to fill my shoes and soak my socks. I ran the next half block, then slowed to a walk. In a front yard on the corner of my block, daffodil buds showed fat and yellow. I felt a poem coming on. By the time I reached my house, I had it.

Squishy, squashy,
Mashy, splashy.
Rainy showers,
Yellow flowers.
I want to sing!
It's almost spring!

The poem felt good—like my mood.

Five

~~~~~

My father called that eve-
ning. Although he and Mom were divorced when I
was in kindergarten, I used to see him every single
weekend. But last year he moved to Washington,
D.C., so now we only visit during vacations. I miss
him a lot.

"Hello, Sport," he said when I answered the
phone. "Sport" is his nickname for me.

"Hi, Dad!"

"You sound in a good mood."

"I am."

"What's happening?"

"I'm going to a party! It's not for a couple of weeks,
but I already have a boy to go with."

"Boy?"

"Jerome Kirksey. He's a neat kid, but he's just a
friend."

"That's good," Dad said.

"Mom and I are going shopping for a fancy dress and shoes," I told him. "I'm going to wear high heels."

"High heels?" Dad sounded absolutely shocked.

"All the girls are wearing them." I tried to sound casual, as if I had a whole closet full of high heels. "I can't wait," I added. "It's been forever since I was in a shoe store."

There was such a long silence on the line that I thought we were cut off. Then he said, "But you hate trying on shoes."

"That was when I was a little kid. I've grown up a lot since I visited you at Christmas."

"It's only been a few months."

"Some people mature faster than others," I told him. "I must have been just about ripe."

I heard something that could have been a laugh. Then Dad said, "I really love you, Chelsea. I wish I could be there to give you a big hug."

"I love you too." I don't know if it was because Dad called me by my real name or because I wanted to see him so much, but tears started in my eyes.

Then Juliet snatched the phone from my hand, almost before I could say good-bye. It's funny, but it seems I miss Dad more when I visit or talk to him than when I don't hear from him at all.

"My father called last night," I announced to the other girls when we met at the lockers the next morning, "and I told him all about the party."

"Did you mention boys?" asked Jill.

"Yes." I tried to keep a smug expression off my face and failed. "I told him I'd invited Jerome."

"You got a date!" said Rachel.

Gina didn't say anything because I'd already told her, but Jill managed a halfhearted, "All right." Danielle looked as if she smelled something bad.

"Why did you ask Jerome?" asked Kendra. She had a sulky expression on her face.

Before I could answer, Danielle butted in. "Because C.R. turned her down flat," she said.

"He had a date with me," said Rachel, sounding as if she and C.R. had been going together a long time.

"You make me so mad, Rachel," I told her. "You knew I wanted to ask C.R."

"After saying he smells like cat dirt?"

"So he has a few drawbacks."

"Chelsea . . ." Kendra tugged at my sleeve. "Why did you invite Jerome?"

"He has a good personality and can be lots of fun."

"Oh," she said. "I thought maybe you liked him."

"Of course not! We're just good friends."

When Kendra's face lost its sulky expression, I wondered if maybe she liked Jerome. I didn't have a chance to find out, not then anyway. Mr. Feeny poked his head outside of Room 14 and told us we were going to be late if we didn't hustle.

Mr. Feeny is the first man I've ever had for a teacher. While he isn't my all-time favorite, he's pretty far up in my personal popularity poll. After I took my seat and got out my health textbook, I eyed him critically. He'd probably look better if he gained ten pounds and shaved off his mustache, I decided.

"All right." Mr. Feeny swung his arms and smacked his hands together, as if he were a coach talking to his team before the big game. "We've covered the skeletal system and the respiratory system. Today we begin the reproductive system."

A current of sound ran through the room, like a gust of air blowing down an empty corridor. I groaned, unfortunately louder than the noises making up the current.

"I sense a lack of enthusiasm, Chelsea." Mr. Feeny smacked his hands together again.

"I already know enough about the reproductive system," I told him.

"Umm. Anyone want to comment on that?" Mr. Feeny looked over the class. "Lindsey?"

Lindsey shook her head. She also turned bright red.

"Hey," said Mr. Feeny. "No cause for embarrassment. We all got here that way."

"My gerbils do it all the time," said Rachel.

"Which is why there are a lot of gerbils in the world." Mr. Feeny paused a couple of seconds, then added, "There are two things every single person on this planet has done or will do. One is to die. What is the other? Class?"

"Be born," said almost everyone.

"Right. Now I know none of you can remember your birth—"

"I can!" said Jerome.

"Please raise your hand," said Mr. Feeny. "Remember it or not, a birth of any kind is a tremendous event."

"I'll say," said Rachel. "My mother gerbil—"

"Rachel! Jerome! Everybody! RAISE YOUR HANDS! If you don't, I'm going to assign a paper on the reproductive system instead of teaching it in class."

Nobody laughed, moaned, groaned, snorted, or did anything to make noise. As for me, I sat absolutely still and held my breath.

When my respiratory system was about to collapse from lack of air, Mr. Feeny said, "Although we were present, most of us don't remember our birth, but we might have heard stories about it. Does anyone have a story to tell us about their birth?"

A lot of kids raised their hands, but I kept mine down. The only story I've heard about my birth is about Juliet's sibling visit to the hospital. When she saw me, she started to cry. "They gave us an ugly one," she said.

Fortunately, I've improved a lot since then.

Mr. Feeny called on Danielle first.

"My aunt's going to have a baby in July and she can't smoke, and can't drink any beer or coffee."

"That's because her body is in the very important business of growing a new human being," said Mr. Feeny. "We'll discuss those things later, but right now we're talking about our own births. Do you have an interesting story, Chad?"

"I was born two minutes after my mother got to the hospital, in the hall outside the emergency room," said Chad. "My father says it's the scariest thing that ever happened to him."

"I can understand that," said Mr. Feeny. "Ryan?"

"I was a blue baby."

"Blue!" Chad laughed. "You from Mars?"

"I was just blue," said Ryan.

"A baby can be born blue because of lack of oxygen," Mr. Feeny explained. "C.R.?"

"When I was born, I was really sick. I had some fluid in my head."

"What was it?"

C.R. thought a couple of seconds. "Water, I guess."

"What did they do?" asked Jerome. "Pump you out?"

I couldn't hear C.R.'s answer because the rest of the kids were laughing. When they stopped, Ryan said, "So that's what happened. I always thought the nurse dropped you on your head."

C.R. leaned out of his seat to punch Ryan on his

shoulder. We all knew Ryan was teasing, because he and C.R. hang around together.

"What about you girls?" Mr. Feeny said. "Don't any of you have a story about your birth?"

Gina, Lindsey, and Jill put up their hands. Mr. Feeny called on Lindsey.

"Our family has a videotape of my sister being born."

"You're kidding," said Rachel.

"No." Lindsey shook her head. "It's of my little sister, Tricia."

"Who took it?" asked Ryan.

"My dad."

"How'd your sister look?" I asked, not raising my hand because nobody else did.

"All yellow and slimy."

"That's embarrassing," said Gina. "Think of when she's grown up and has a boyfriend . . ."

"Yeah," Jerome said. "Like it's after Thanksgiving dinner, and everyone's sitting around, trying to digest their turkey and pumpkin pie. Then up pops Lindsey's dad with the video."

"Gross," said Danielle.

"Bring it in so we can watch it," I said.

Everyone laughed.

"I'm serious," I protested. "It would be neat to see a baby being born."

"Yes it would, Chelsea," said Mr. Feeny. "However, birth is a very private experience, which might be why the other students laughed." He paused to look around the room. "Some of you might find discussing reproduction difficult, especially in a mixed group. So we're going to cover subjects like emotional changes and new feelings together. For information on the physical side of puberty, the girls will go to Mrs. Rudolph in Room 12. I'll teach the boys from her class, along with the guys in here."

That was a relief. I'd rather learn about sexual changes from a woman teacher, if I had to learn about them at all. Just the thought of puberty made me nervous, maybe because it meant I was growing up—ready or not.

Suddenly my stomach felt queasy. I stole a look at Gina and then at Lindsey, who sits catty-cornered in front of her. They didn't look embarrassed or upset or anything. They looked exactly the same as they had when we learned about the respiratory system, except a little more curious.

"Now," said Mr. Feeny, "I am going to have Lanie pass out a paper for you to take home to your parents.

It gives a brief summary of some of the topics you'll be studying, and has a place for either your mother or your father to sign. I need it back in two days. Any questions?"

Nobody had any, or at least they didn't want to ask them out loud.

"Puberty is the period of growth when a male or female first becomes able to make a new human being," Mr. Feeny told us.

I rolled the paper Lanie gave me between my fingers, wishing I could make it into a paper airplane and fly it away in the March wind. My queasy stomach lurched, and I decided I hadn't been very smart to add chips and a donut to the sandwich and apple in my lunch bag. Maybe they were what was making me feel yucky. Or maybe it was puberty.

"During these physical changes, boys and girls are bombarded by a whole series of strong emotions. One minute you feel as if you're going to cry, and the next you're laughing with your friends. What are some other strong emotions you are feeling these days? Chad?"

"Sometimes I get really mad."

"That's very common," said Mr. Feeny. "What about you, Jerome?"

44

"I want to do the things I want to do," said Jerome, "and not have my parents order me around."

"A desire for independence." Mr. Feeny wrote that and *bursts of anger* on the board.

I rolled the paper tighter.

"Jill," he said, "what are you feeling right now?"

"Kind of curious, I guess."

Mr. Feeny wrote again. Then he asked, "And what does puberty make you feel like, Chelsea?"

Unfortunately, I didn't give myself a chance to think. The words popped out of my mouth before I could stop them.

"Sick to my stomach," I said.

Everybody laughed. Even Mr. Feeny couldn't stop a big smile from creeping across his face. I'd told the truth—and turned into the class clown.

Six

After waiting five minutes for Gina the next morning, I decided she wasn't coming and went on to school. The hall near Room 14 was empty except for Jerome, who was standing near my locker.

"I want to talk to you," he said.

"So talk." I shoved my coat and book bag into the locker, took out the notebook and books I needed, and headed toward the classroom. Jerome trailed after me.

"Kendra wants me to go to the party with her."

So that was why she'd acted sulky. I paused at the door of our room. If the late bell sounded, we could run inside and throw ourselves in our seats before Mr. Feeny could take attendance.

"But you'd already asked me," said Jerome.

"Right. I asked you *first*."

Jerome shifted from one foot to the other. "I

figured if I told you I want to go to the party with Kendra, you'd be a good sport and uninvite me."

"No way." I shook my head. I wasn't going through inviting another boy.

"Please, Chelsea."

"Why do you want to go with Kendra instead of me?"

"I'm almost as tall as she is."

"That's no reason." Most of the kids were in their seats, and Mr. Feeny was staring toward the hall. It had to be time for the bell.

"Kendra's prettier than you are."

"Thanks a million, Jerome." I pushed by him and went through the doorway. "But I invited you first, and I'm not going to uninvite you."

My bottom hit the seat of my chair as the bell sounded. Since Gina still hadn't appeared, I figured she was sick. But five minutes later, she and Ryan came into the room together.

"Overslept," she whispered to me as she slid into her seat.

"Did you do it?" I whispered back. I didn't have to explain what "it" was since Gina'd already told me she was going to invite Chad to the party.

She shook her head and put a finger to her lips, then opened her math book.

I heard a little sigh from behind me and twisted in my seat to look at Kendra.

Kendra really is prettier than I am. She has smooth caramel-colored skin and a big beautiful smile. Her large, dark-brown eyes met mine, then shifted over my head.

I turned toward the front of the room.

Mr. Feeny was watching me. His arms were crossed over his middle, and he had a tired expression on his thin face.

I hunched over my book. I *hate* fractions.

I didn't have a chance to talk to Gina until recess. "I tried to call you a million times last night and your line was always busy," I told her.

"My parents were on the phone with my brother," she said. "He wants to quit college."

"Did you invite Chad?" I asked.

"Yes, but he can't go with me because Kendra asked him."

We stopped near the tetherball pole. The pole looked cold and lonely without the orange ball that hangs on it when the weather warms up. "Why did she ask Chad?"

"I don't know."

Kendra, who'd been standing close by with Rachel and Danielle, must have overheard. She walked over to us, locked hands around the tetherball pole, and hugged herself against it. "I asked Chad because you asked Jerome, Chelsea," she said. "And Jerome's mother is making him go with you since you have first dibs."

"Why didn't you invite Anthony or Dominik?"

" 'Cause Anthony is my cousin and I can't stand Dominik." Kendra made a sour face. "All he ever wants to talk about is karate and kung fu."

Rachel, who'd approached with Danielle while Kendra was speaking, asked, "Who are you bringing to my party, Gina?"

"Ryan. I met him on the way into school this morning, and he offered to come with me."

"Super!" I said, wondering why Gina didn't sound more enthusiastic.

"Wait a minute," said Danielle. "Ryan told me he was going to see his aunt in New York that weekend."

Gina shrugged. "Maybe the visit was called off."

"Then he should go to the party with me," said Danielle. "I asked him first."

Gina pulled her lower lip into her mouth, making a little sucking sound.

Danielle stuck out her pointy little chin and narrowed her eyes at Gina. "In reality," she said, "I think *you* asked Ryan and don't want to admit it."

"What's the big deal?" I said. "It doesn't matter what boy we take to the party. We'll all be together once we get there."

Four pairs of angry eyes looked at me.

"You know, like eating french fries, a burger, and a milk shake," I explained. "They all end up in the same place."

"Well, *I* don't think it's fair," said Danielle.

"If you want to get mad at someone, get mad at Rachel," I blurted. "She's the one who dreamed up the idea of inviting boys!"

When Rachel's eyes filled with tears, I opened my mouth to apologize—too late. Danielle took hold of her wrist and pulled her away from the rest of us. "Come on, Rachel," she said. "We know when we're not wanted."

When Gina, Kendra, and I entered Room 14 after recess, Rachel was at Mr. Feeny's desk. Although I tried, I couldn't hear what she was saying as I passed them. I only hoped she wasn't telling on me.

As the rest of us took our seats, Mr. Feeny said, "We're going to work on our science projects, but first we're holding a class meeting at Rachel's request. She'll be in charge." Then Mr. Feeny went to sit at the table at the back of the room.

Rachel must not have known she was going to talk in front of the class that day because she was wearing an old pink shirt with jeans that were too tight in the waist and had a dark green stain on one knee. She looked as if she'd rather hide under the teacher's desk than stand beside it. "I want to explain about my birthday party," she said in a shaky voice.

I hadn't realized there was any noise in the room until it stopped. All the little shuffling sounds, the rustle of paper, and the scuffling of feet ceased.

Rachel licked her lips. "My mother promised that I could have a birthday party when I was in the fifth grade," she said, "but the party has to be inside because it's cold and rains a lot in March." She took a deep breath and added, "We don't have a very big house."

That was true. I've been inside Rachel's house many times and it is small. On rainy days we used to play in her basement, which is crammed with all the stuff that won't fit in the rest of the house. We'd pretend it was a maze, before Rachel got to be boy crazy and I became best friends with Gina.

"Mom gave me permission to invite twenty people, but there are thirty-two kids in here." Rachel blinked her eyes rapidly as if she were trying not to cry. "I didn't want to leave anybody out."

I looked down at my desktop. My left hand had a streak of ballpoint-pen ink across the palm. I rubbed slowly at the streak, thinking how hard it must have been for Rachel to decide whom to invite and whom to leave out.

"My stepfather suggested I invite the girls since there are ten of us, and have each girl invite a boy. That way nobody would think I don't like them."

Chad's hand shot up. When Rachel called on him, he said, "Why didn't you find out who the other girls wanted and invite them yourself?"

"Then the boys who weren't invited would be mad at me."

Lindsey waved her hand.

"Lindsey?" said Rachel.

"It's only a birthday party. Nobody's going to be mad at you, especially now that they know why you did it that way."

Rachel smiled at Lindsey, as if to say "thanks." I

thought of something else that might make her feel better and raised my hand.

When she called on me, I told her, "I don't see what all the fuss is about. It's not as if any of us is going on a real date."

I should have realized when Rachel called on Danielle next that there was trouble headed my way, but I didn't.

"In reality," said Danielle, "this *is* practice for a real date. Grow up, Chelsea."

"In reality," I shot right back at her, "I'll be eighteen in seven years. I can be grown up the rest of my life."

"What a nerd."

At the back of the room, Mr. Feeny cleared his throat, but he didn't interrupt.

"I don't understand why you're always so mean to me," I told Danielle. "I never did a single thing to you."

"Haven't you ever heard of Operation Tough Love?" Danielle is a pretty girl, but when she sneers, she looks ugly.

"What's Operation Tough Love?" asked Kendra.

"It's when you really care about a person, so you tell them about their mistakes even if they hate you for it," Danielle explained. "You have to be tough. Make them listen so they don't wreck their lives."

"You mean *you* love *me?*" I put one finger in my mouth and pretended to barf.

"See?" said Danielle. "Chelsea can't admit that she's wrong."

"Because I'm not," I told her. Then I realized Rachel, Lindsey, Chad, and most of the rest of the class had *Oh, yeah?* expressions on their faces. "So what am I supposed to do?" I demanded.

Jerome jumped partway out of his seat, waving his hand.

Rachel called on him even though Chad was already talking.

"Unask me!" said Jerome. "Please, Chelsea."

"If you unask Jerome, I'll unask Chad," Kendra said.

"And I'll unask Ryan," offered Gina.

"Then I can invite Ryan and everybody will be happy," said Danielle.

I tried stalling, but that wasn't easy with the other kids waiting for my answer. I glanced at Mr. Feeny, but the blank expression on his face didn't help. "All right," I agreed. "You're unasked, Jerome."

"Way to go!" said Chad.

Ryan groaned and buried his face in his arms. The other kids acted as if they were pleased with the new arrangement. Even the boys who weren't invited to the party didn't seem to care since they understood why Rachel hadn't asked them.

Everyone was happy—except me.

Seven

~~~~~

Mom was on the telephone when I burst into the kitchen. At the sight of my face she said, "I'll talk to you later," and hung up. She pushed the phone to one side on the counter and rested her arms in front of her.

"Who were you talking to?" I asked.

"Nobody," Mom said in a tone that meant, "I don't want to tell you."

I raised my eyebrow.

"Just a man."

"*Just* a man?"

"Well . . . maybe a boyfriend."

"I don't believe it!" I had a vision of Mom kissing someone good night at our front door, and I banged a fist on the counter. "Why do you need a boyfriend?"

"I don't *need* a boyfriend," she told me, "but it would be nice to go out with a member of the opposite sex once in a while."

When I groaned, Mom added, "You can't be this crabby just because I was talking to a man on the phone. What happened?"

"Turns out Jerome and Kendra like each other," I told her, "so I was practically forced to uninvite Jerome to the party."

"Oh . . ." Understanding filled Mom's eyes, and she reached to touch my arm. "That's too bad."

"Now I don't have anyone to go with."

"There are plenty of other boys."

"That's not everything. Danielle Rogers embarrassed me in front of the whole class. She called me a nerd. And a few days ago she said I was socially retarded." I stared at a series of small marks on the countertop.

"Listen to me, Chelsea." Mom's voice was tense, as if she might be ready to give one of her lectures. I licked my lips, then pressed them tightly together.

"You are not socially retarded," she said. "It's silly for Danielle to even think that. There are plenty of girls who never have a boyfriend until they're out of high school, and they're not socially retarded either."

That made me feel a little bit better. Unfortunately, Mom went and ruined it by adding, "But I'm really happy you're starting to learn about boy-girl relationships now. It's a lot easier when you're young."

Easier! How could Mom say that? Didn't she remember what it was like to be in the fifth grade?

That was when Juliet came into the kitchen and opened the refrigerator. She took out the container she keeps filled with cut-up carrots and celery. As she climbed onto the stool next to Mom's, she asked, "What's wrong now?"

"She's without a boy for the party again," said Mom.

"Is that all?" Juliet selected a stick of celery and began to munch on it.

"Life is so unfair," I complained.

"You're only finding out now?" Juliet is usually more sympathetic. She must have failed another geometry test.

"It's not as if I ask for much," I told her. "All I want is to be like the other kids."

"You mean you want the other kids to be like you," said Juliet.

"I DO NOT!"

Mom frowned, but I ignored her.

"If I don't go to that party, Danielle will spend the

entire time talking about me," I said. "Besides, I don't want to miss all the fun."

"I'll dress like a boy and you can take me," Juliet offered.

"That's a great idea!"

"Wrong," said Mom. "It's a bad idea and I won't permit it."

"Oh, joy." I helped myself to one of Juliet's carrot sticks. The carrot was cool and crunchy, but it lacked the comfort value of a chocolate-chip cookie.

For a few minutes the kitchen was silent except for the crunch of carrots and the hum of the refrigerator.

"I'll get you a date," said Juliet.

"Not a date," I protested. "All I want is a warm body to get me through the door at Rachel's house."

"You can go with Marty's brother, Shawn."

"Marty has a brother?"

"He has two," said Juliet. "The younger one's a pain, but Shawn's a nice kid. He's in the seventh grade."

"Is he taller than I am?"

"Definitely."

"What's he look like?"

"He's cute. He has black hair and the darkest blue eyes I've ever seen, almost navy."

I pictured walking into Rachel's party with a tall, good-looking stranger who was practically in the eighth grade, and my spirits rose. Danielle would pass out from jealousy. "What makes you think he'll go with me?" I asked.

"He will." Juliet sounded so confident that she aroused my suspicions.

"I want to see a picture of him," I said.

"I don't have one." Juliet dug into her vegetable supply and pulled out a piece of celery with small leaves attached.

"He probably looks like Bigfoot," I muttered. "But then I'm not exactly a beauty queen either."

"Don't be so hard on yourself," said Mom. "You're a pretty girl."

"I'm a complete klutz."

"All you need is a little help." She studied me. "With a new dress and a few lessons in how to act at a grown-up party—"

"An operation sewing my mouth shut."

"You'll be the belle of the ball," Mom said firmly.

That sounded almost as bad as being socially retarded.

"How about it?" asked Juliet.

I was clearly outnumbered, but I shook my head.

"Hey, come on," said Juliet. "I'll try to get you a picture, but take my word for it. This kid is tall and cute, and he likes the same things you do—frogs and toads . . . spiders, lizards."

I eyed her doubtfully.

"Trust me," said Juliet. She nodded her head, her fringe of blond curls bobbing enthusiastically.

I looked at Mom, who smiled encouragingly.

I didn't exactly have boys standing in line, hoping for me to invite them to the party. "All right," I said, giving in. "But I get to see a picture first."

"No problem," Juliet agreed with great good cheer.

Trust me. No problem. I felt a surge of optimism. With a handsome older boy, I'd be the envy of all the other girls. Then Danielle Rogers would see who needed Operation Tough Love.

Eight

~~~~~~

When I woke up on Satur-
day, rain was beating on the porch roof outside my
window. The morning was a total loss, unless I
counted working on my VIP paper. I wrote: *The
mountain gorillas were always in danger when Dian
wasn't at the research camp, so she decided to live at
Karisoke. Instead of living in comfort in the United States,
she stayed in the cold, wet jungle.*

The books I'd checked out of the library had a lot
of photographs of gorillas and of the area around
Dian's camp. I studied them, listening to the sound
of water on the roof and thinking how horrible it
would be to live in a rain forest. In order to do that,
Dian Fossey had to care about the gorillas more than
anything else in the world.

After I finished working on my report, I spent ten
or fifteen minutes messing around on the piano.

None of those minutes were very much fun for me. It's unreal that Gina can practice every single day.

"I'm going out," I told Mom, when the downpour stopped early in the afternoon.

"Where?"

"To Gina's."

"You'd better call her first. She might not be home."

"If she isn't, I'll stop at Lindsey Matta's."

"Don't forget to wear a jacket."

I pulled an old red sweatshirt of Juliet's over my head. The front of the sweatshirt was plain, but the back had a big picture of Minnie Mouse printed on it. The black of Minnie's ears was beginning to fade.

Since Juliet likes her sweatshirts huge, the shirt was very long, almost to my knees. I rolled up the cuffs, then ran a comb through my hair, retied my right sneaker, and headed for Gina's house, rolling the sweatshirt sleeves higher as I walked.

When Gina wasn't home, I crossed the street and headed toward Lindsey's house.

A robin sang in a big old maple near the corner of the block. The trees were covered with fat buds, and purple crocuses bloomed under a yew bush. The air smelled fresh and clean. I took a deep breath and stared at the sky as I walked.

The only clouds left after the rain were fluffy white ones. They chased each other across a bright-blue background, changing shape as they went. A large, round ghost transformed itself into a dog's head with floppy ears, and then into a pirate ship.

I ought to write a poem about clouds, I thought. Then I tripped on a raised piece of sidewalk and almost fell flat on my face. After that I concentrated on my feet instead of the sky. I rounded another corner and could see Lindsey's house.

C.R., who lives near Lindsey, was playing Frisbee with Ryan on the sidewalk out front. Circling them, I went to sit beside Lindsey on her steps. I leaned back to rest my elbows on the small square of cement that is her porch. Although the steps didn't look wet, they felt cold and damp through my jeans.

"I once saw a dog who could catch a Frisbee," I said as we watched Ryan throw the orange disc toward C.R.

C.R. stretched for the toss, displaying a strip of bare skin between the top of his purple sweats and the bottoms. A faded streak, maybe from spilled bleach, made a jagged blur of white on the top, and the bottoms hung baggy through the knees. He glanced at me, then threw the Frisbee to Ryan.

I shifted on the damp cement, afraid that C.R. was remembering the ugly things I'd said about him.

"Where's Gina?" Lindsey asked me.

"In Cleveland, practicing with the orchestra."

"I used to play the piano, but I wasn't very good at it," Lindsey said.

Ryan ran close to the steps to capture the disc after one of C.R.'s wilder throws. His black sweatshirt was even messier than C.R.'s and had its sleeves ripped off. "Let's play keep-away," he suggested.

"We don't have anyone to keep it from," said C.R.

"Them." Ryan jerked his head toward Lindsey and me.

"Right." C.R. sounded pleased by the idea. "How 'bout it, Lindsey?"

"If Chelsea wants to."

"Sure!"

"Think fast!" Ryan twisted, folding one arm behind his back to flip the Frisbee to C.R.

"Got it." C.R. held the Frisbee over his head as Lindsey tried to grab it.

Ryan ran back several yards, then jumped to catch the toss C.R. aimed in his direction. He missed, his hand deflecting the disc.

I charged from my position near the steps, but C.R. was closer. He practically grabbed the Frisbee from my hands and danced away, laughing at me. He wagged the disc at me, then turned and ran. I ran after him, catching up before he reached the corner.

We played hide-and-seek around the mailbox until Ryan was close enough for C.R. to throw the disc in his direction.

Lindsey had her fingers on the Frisbee when Ryan grabbed it.

"Foul!" I shouted.

"No way," said C.R.

"Cheaters," I returned.

Ryan launched another shot in C.R.'s direction. Like the last one, it went wild, only this time I was closer than C.R. I chased the rolling orange disc across the street, over a culvert, and across the curb lawn, then down the sidewalk, with C.R. close behind me.

"Got it," I grunted, scooping up the slippery plastic.

"Got *you*." C.R. grabbed me around the waist.

"Let go!" I leaned forward, hoping to get a clear shot at Lindsey, but one foot slipped in the mud. C.R. and I went tumbling.

"Gimme." As he rolled free, C.R. grabbed one side of the Frisbee with both hands.

I sat up and held on, staring from a distance of about six inches into C.R.'s sky-blue eyes. He had mud caked along one side of his head, but he smelled wonderful—like earth, fresh green grass, and laundry that's been dried in the sun.

C.R. must be a mind reader, because suddenly he grinned at me and said, "Cat dirt, huh?"

"I'm sorry!"

C.R. laughed, letting go of the disc at the same time. I landed flat on my back, still clutching the Frisbee.

Two dark silhouettes appeared between me and the sky. I thought they belonged to Ryan and Lindsey, but when I sat up, I found out different.

Danielle and Rachel were staring down at me. Rachel looked confused, but Danielle was wearing her superior expression. Both girls were totally clean, as if they'd never gone near a mud puddle in their entire lives.

"I told you so," Danielle said to Rachel.

I checked my arm, legs, and body. They were grass-stained and smeared with mud. My hands were mud-covered too.

"What did you tell her?" I asked as I wiped my hands on the wet grass.

"That you and C. R. were at Lindsey's house . . ." Danielle paused, then added significantly, "together."

"So what?" I looked around, but C. R. and Ryan had vanished. Lindsey was sitting on the porch steps, wiping mud off her sneakers with a tissue.

"*You* know what," said Danielle, "boy stealer." She put an arm around Rachel and led her away, as if from the scene of a bad accident.

"Don't worry, Rachel," she said, glancing back over a shoulder at me, then looking at Rachel. "In reality, Chelsea's nothing but a child. She'll never be able to take C. R. from you."

I staggered to my feet. My shoes were two misshapen clumps of mud. "Hey, Rachel," I called after them. "I wasn't trying to steal C. R. Honest! I was only trying to hang on to the Frisbee!"

Maybe Rachel would have listened to me if she'd

been alone. Maybe. As it was, she and Danielle acted as if they didn't hear a word I said. The two of them marched off, their backs turned toward me, as if neither one wanted a thing to do with me—ever.

Nine

~~~~~~

How did one person steal another person? Unless the thief was a kidnapper, of course. I mean, C.R. wasn't a candy bar or a wallet.

I almost hoped Rachel would uninvite me to her party over the C.R.-stealing business, since that would solve my boy problem. But then Juliet brought home a picture of Marty's brother, and I decided I didn't have a boy problem after all.

The photograph was a head-and-shoulders shot from a school yearbook, so I couldn't tell how tall Shawn was, but he definitely was good-looking. Even I, who am not an expert on boys, knew the sight of him would turn the other girls green.

"I have to give it back," Juliet told me when I put the photograph in my wallet.

"Can I keep it a couple of days?"

When Juliet hesitated, I assumed a sad puppy expression and added, "Please?"

"All right." Juliet is a real softy at heart. "But don't let anything happen to it."

I was so happy with Shawn's picture that I could hardly wait until Monday. When I showed it to Gina Sunday afternoon, she whistled. Then she said, "I'd uninvite Chad for him."

"Don't tell anyone Juliet found him for me," I cautioned. "He's going to be my mysterious older boy."

"Okay," said Gina. "You deserve a break."

I deserved a bunch of breaks, but I wasn't going to complain about the one I got. I guarded the photograph and waited for the perfect moment to show it to the other girls on Monday.

The moment didn't come until recess. Before that, we girls went to Mrs. Rudolph's room to learn more about reproduction. Mrs. Rudolph began our lesson by mentioning we'd already studied some of the larger physical elements involved in reproduction and now it was time to learn about the tiniest.

"Small but mighty," she told us. "Chromosomes and genes are very important elements in establishing the physical and mental characteristics of a new human being.

"Jill, read aloud the section on chromosomes on

page thirty of the workbook," she said. "The rest of you follow silently."

It turned out that chromosomes were very interesting and not embarrassing at all. They contained genes, which gave instructions to the cells on how to grow and develop—like whether to have grayish-blue eyes and brown hair like me, or green eyes and reddish hair like Gina.

I started daydreaming about building a human being, and then about changing animals that already exist. When the other girls left for recess, I stayed behind to ask Mrs. Rudolph if scientists could design animals, if they could make a sparrow sing like a canary or put black-and-white zebra stripes on a pony.

Mrs. Rudolph said such experiments were being performed on more simple forms of animal life. "It's a very controversial issue," she told me, "as many people, including some scientists, believe such experiments are potentially dangerous."

Thinking of all kinds of wonderful new animals, I went to join the other girls, who had gathered near the outside wall of the building. Rachel was looking at her reflection in a window. Lanie was moaning about zits. I didn't understand what the fuss was about, since Lanie only had a couple.

"Well, *I* have pubic hair," announced Rachel, still staring at herself in the window.

"It looks fine to me," I said.

There was a second's silence. Then everyone laughed.

"That was a joke!" I yelled, remembering too late what pubic hair is. Trying to change the subject, I added, "I was just talking with Mrs. Rudolph. She said someday it might be possible to make ponies striped like zebras."

Between giggles, Lanie said, "That's weird."

"Zebras aren't weird," I protested.

"They are if their genes are mixed with ponies'," Jill pointed out. Her eyes narrowed and she smiled as if she'd thought of something very clever. "That's what you are, Chelsea," she said, "a zebra."

"A zebra?" I echoed, not getting what she meant.

"Yeah. Zebra Zeller—a zebra in a herd of ponies!"

"No, I'm not! I'm just like everybody else!"

"If you're like everyone else," said Danielle, sticking her pointy little chin out at me, "who are you taking to the party?"

"I have somebody." My spirits rose. This was the perfect moment to bring up Shawn.

"Sure you do," said Danielle. "You have boys begging to go with you, all the fifth grade and half the fourth."

"I wouldn't invite those little kids," I said scornfully. "I'd feel like a baby-sitter."

"You don't have to bring a boy from our school," said Rachel, who might be boy crazy but is still good-hearted.

"That's super," I said, "because I called Shawn last night. He's been dying to go out with me, but my Dad's so old-fashioned. He wants me to be in high school before I date." I shrugged casually. "I'm lucky Mom claims Rachel's party isn't a date."

"Who's Shawn?" demanded Danielle.

"A guy I know." As my eyes met Gina's, I resisted the urge to wink. Gina began to giggle, but managed to control herself before any of the other girls noticed.

"Oh, sure." Danielle put her fists on her skinny hips. "I think he's somebody who doesn't exist."

"You are so wrong," I told her. "I can show you his picture, and I'll show him to you in person at the party."

"Do you have his picture with you?" asked Kendra.

"Right here." I found my wallet among the tissues, gum wrappers, and other junk in my coat pocket. I took the photograph out and held it up for the other girls to see.

"Cute," breathed Rachel, who would think any boy was cute as long as he didn't have two noses.

"He's practically the best-looking boy I've ever seen," said Gina.

Jill snatched the photograph from me. She glanced at it, then passed it to Danielle. "So what's he want with you?" she demanded.

"A date. He's practically in the eighth grade. I must appeal to older boys."

"How?" asked Rachel. Her cheeks flushed pink and she added, "I didn't mean that as a put-down."

"Shawn likes the way I'm natural, myself," I explained, "instead of trying to act like somebody I'm not." I reached for the photograph, but Danielle moved it out of my reach.

For a second I was afraid she might tear it up. "Give me back that picture," I said. "It's the only one I have."

Danielle scowled, but she handed over the photo-graph.

I looked at it lovingly and sighed. "My dad will be furious when he finds out about Shawn," I said dramatically, "but I don't care. I just want to be near him."

"Are you that serious?" Kendra's eyes were so innocent and trusting that I felt guilty.

No way could I let a little guilt wreck my act. "I don't know how serious I am," I said slowly, "but Shawn's been crazy about me for a long time." I hesitated, then went on. "I hate to be sneaky, so we've never gone out together. Maybe I don't actually know him at all."

"If you decide you don't want him," said Rachel, "you can give him to me."

"I'll think about it," I promised. Then I laughed. I couldn't help it.

"What's so funny?" asked Kendra, but I shook my head. I didn't want to hurt anybody's feelings, so I kept my thought to myself.

I'd just come up with the perfect birthday present for Rachel—a boy.

T e n

I couldn't give Rachel a boy for her birthday; I'd already bought her a gift, an ant farm. I'd wanted one for years.

"Remember when I made my own ant farm in the first grade?" I asked Mom, "and how mad you were when the ants escaped?"

"Most of them ended up in the kitchen," she said, doubtfully eyeing the farm. "I do wish you'd let Rachel send away for the ants instead of getting them yourself."

Behind a layer of glass, the ants were going about their business, carrying crumbs of dirt out of their excavation, tending the little white beads of babies. Mom folded a double layer of gift wrap around the farm and taped it.

"Those ants don't have to worry about a thing," I observed. "Their whole lives are arranged so they never once get sweaty armpits."

"I'm not so certain about that." Mom fastened a large pink bow to the front of the package, then twisted on the couch to look out the front window. "Juliet should be back here by now," she said. "I hope nothing's happened."

Juliet and Marty had gone to his house to pick up Shawn. "Me too," I said. I paced the living-room carpet, practicing walking in high heels. "Maybe they stopped somewhere so Shawn could buy me a corsage."

"I doubt it," said Mom. "Don't *clump* like that, Chelsea. And remember, your feet are supposed to point the same direction."

"Oh. Right." I should have bought the lower heels that Mom had suggested. They would have been easier to walk in. I tugged at my stockings. "I *hate* panty hose!"

Mom sighed. "Well, try not to pull at your underwear like a baseball player."

I practiced walking with my toes pointed the same direction. My shoes seemed to grow tighter and tighter as I practiced. Soon every toe felt as if it were being amputated.

What was a little pain in exchange for convincing the other girls I was like them? Besides, lots of women wear panty hose and tight shoes every day of their lives. I sure hoped that wasn't going to be part of *my* future.

I paced some more, trying to hide the fact I was worried. What if Shawn had demanded to see a picture of me? What if he found out I was a zebra instead of a pony? What if he backed out? I glanced at my mother.

Much to my surprise, Mom was fidgeting, squirming on the couch and twisting a loop of pink ribbon between her fingers.

What does she have to be nervous about? I wondered. I'm the one who's going to the party.

The phone rang.

I ran to answer it, tripped, and grabbed the phone's cord as I fell. The phone landed on top of me. "Hello!" I shouted. "Hello, hello!"

"Hello," said someone on the other end of the line, a girl. In my nervousness, I couldn't tell if she was Juliet or not.

"Hello!" I shouted again.

"Is this Chelsea?"

"Yes."

"This is Danielle."

"Oh." I rolled over and sat up, stretching my legs

in front of me and eyeing the blue shoes at the end of them. You'd think the people who manufacture shoes would know women's feet are shaped the same as men's. The toes of my shoes were narrow and pointed instead of wide, like my foot.

"All the kids are here except you," Danielle said, "and we're wondering if you were sick."

I covered the phone's mouthpiece with my hand. "If Juliet messes up, I will *exterminate* her," I whispered aloud.

"They're here!" Mom called from the living room. "They've just pulled up!"

I lifted my palm from the phone. "We're leaving any minute now," I said sweetly. "We were talking and completely forgot about the party until Mom reminded us." Then I hung up before Danielle could ask any more questions.

"They seem to be waiting for you to come out," observed Mom when I returned to the living room.

"Let them wait." I crossed to the nearest chair and flopped in it. "They're the ones who were late."

"Please, Chelsea, sit with your knees together when you wear a skirt."

The shoes didn't hurt nearly as much when I was

sitting, and the blue of them matched the blue of the smooth-fitting top we'd bought at the mall. My skirt was a darker blue and fell in soft folds to my knees.

I put up a hand to touch my hair. As a result of a lot of work with a curling iron and hair spray, it formed large, dark-brown waves. They made my face seem longer and my eyes larger. I actually looked quite pretty—for me.

Mom motioned for Juliet and the boys to come to the house. "Don't forget," she told me, "the whole idea of a party is to enjoy yourself."

Not this party. This party was my chance to prove I was like the other girls. I gave one last tug to my panty hose. Then the front door opened and Juliet came into the living room, followed by Marty and Shawn.

As he shut the door behind him, Shawn glanced around the room, his eyes finally stopping on me. He was wearing a baggy tan jacket over a light-green shirt and dark-brown pants. The pants were too short, revealing black Reeboks and what I suspected were bare ankles. He was very short.

My nervousness vanished along with any hope of impressing the other girls. Shawn looked pretty young for a boy who was practically in the eighth grade. As a matter of fact, he looked young for a kid in the fifth grade.

I closed my eyes. When I opened them again, Shawn hadn't improved any.

"Are you ready?" asked Juliet.

I didn't answer. I should have known better than to trust her.

"Shawn, this is Chelsea," she said.

Shawn smiled. Actually, it was more of a smirk, the middle of his lips pressed together and the ends turned up. Although his hair was dark like it was in the photograph, it was cut very close to his head. His eyes hinted at the same smirk as his mouth, and his skin was pasty white. The best thing about him was that he was clean.

I stood and went closer to get a better look.

"Do you always walk that way?" he asked.

"Come here, Juliet." I clumped back across the living room, through the dining room, and into the kitchen. After a couple of seconds, Juliet joined me.

"He's shorter than me!" I hissed.

"So slump a little."

"Four inches?"

Juliet bit her lower lip.

"And he doesn't look at all like his picture."

"He's a boy, isn't he?"

I gritted my teeth, trying to decide which would be worse: showing up at the party with a child, or not showing up at all.

I opted for going with short Shawn. "Tell him I'll be there in a minute," I said.

I kicked off my blue heels and ran upstairs to my bedroom, where I dug an old pair of black sandals out of my closet. Before putting on the sandals, I stripped off my panty hose. If Shawn didn't bother with stockings, why should I?

Before going back downstairs, I stopped in Juliet's room to borrow her sunglasses.

"I'm ready," I announced as I entered the living room.

"Why are you wearing sunglasses?" asked Marty.

"I was rubbing my eyes and I don't want the other kids to think I have pinkeye."

"Have a good time," Mom told us as we left the house. She didn't sound as if she considered it very likely.

Shawn hadn't grown any taller while I was in the bedroom. And, as we reached the sidewalk, I could have sworn something moved in one of his jacket pockets. He shoved a hand in the pocket and the movement stopped.

Halfway to the car, I heard Mom yell after me. I turned and went back to the porch, where she was holding Rachel's present. "You forgot the ant farm," she said.

"An ant farm!" said Shawn. "Neato."

Neato. Wait till Danielle heard that. I briefly considered killing Juliet *before* the party.

"You know," said Shawn, "you don't look at all like your picture."

Eleven

~~~~~~~~~~

The back of Marty's car smelled as if he had a part-time job hauling wet dogs. I figured that in a matter of minutes I'd smell like a wet dog too, but I didn't care. Nobody would notice my aroma; they'd be too busy eyeballing Shawn.

Although Rachel's house is only five blocks from mine, the ride seemed to take forever. I slouched in the backseat beside Shawn, listening to the odd little quacking noises he was making and imagining the jokes the other kids would make about me for the rest of the school year. Not only would I look like a total nerd in front of all the girls in Room 14, but half the boys too.

As the quacking noises increased, I tried to see if Shawn was moving his lips, but it was too dark in the backseat of the car. "We don't have to hang around together after we get to the party," I pointed out. "I have lots of friends I'm going to want to talk to."

"Neato," he said cheerfully.

I hunched over, wrapping my arms around my waist and beginning to work up a good pretense of a stomachache.

The quacking noise was louder near the seat. I straightened, then hunched again to check it out.

"Here we are," Juliet announced as Marty pulled to the curb in front of Rachel's house. She bounced out of the car and held the front seat back for Shawn to get out.

Shawn blocked the opening as he stared at the bunch of balloons the Porters had tied to the porch railing. "Neato," he said again.

I shoved him out of the way and crawled out of the backseat, dragging the ant farm with me. I also gave Juliet the full wattage of my most deadly glare.

"Have fun!" she said.

I choked.

"I know you will," she added, hugging me. "Your first grown-up party!" Juliet sounded exactly like Mom.

"Pick us up early," I told her, then yelled, "Wait!" to Shawn, who was already headed for the house. I ran a few steps, grabbed him with the hand that wasn't carrying the ant farm, and dragged him behind the bushes by Rachel's front porch.

"You have to promise something," I said.

"What?"

"Not to say 'neato' during the party."

"Why not?"

"Because if you say it even once, I'm going to shove your teeth down your throat."

That was when the front door opened and Mrs. Porter appeared. "I thought I heard a car stop," she said. When Shawn stepped back onto the sidewalk, she added, "Oh, there you are."

"Promise?" I hissed at Shawn.

"Okeydokey."

"You're just in time," Mrs. Porter told us. "Rachel's opening her gifts."

"Where?" I looked around, but there were no other kids to be seen.

"In our new family room. Go on through the kitchen. Rachel's aunt Ginger will show you the way."

Aunt Ginger was standing by the door to the basement. "Don't you want to take off your sunglasses?" she asked me.

"No."

"Then be careful on the steps."

It was a good thing she warned me, since I practically had to feel my way to the basement. If the new family room had been any darker, Rachel could have held a cave party. That was all right with me. Maybe nobody else would get a good look at Shawn.

Rachel was sitting in the middle of the room in a pool of bright light from a ceiling fixture. She was surrounded by piles of presents and the remains of wrapping paper and bows. As I worked my way through the crowd, I checked out her gifts: a new umbrella, a fancy sweater, a couple of bracelets, perfume—dumb stuff like that.

Rachel squealed as she opened a small package. "Oh, Jill," she said, hugging a CD to the front of her flowered dress. "Just what I wanted!"

"Happy birthday," I said, giving her the ant farm.

Rachel tore off the pink bow. As she attacked the paper, she said, "Oh, Chelsea, just what I . . . what . . . what is it?"

"An ant farm."

For a second Rachel looked repulsed, but she recovered quickly. "Thank you," she said politely.

"My sister has one of those." Chad pushed between

Gina and Jill. "You should see what happens when I shake it. Those ants go crazy! They're so dumb they think there's an earthquake."

Gina slipped behind Lindsey to stand next to me. "I wish Kendra had never uninvited him," she whispered. "I was better off with Ryan."

My present had been the last. As Rachel stood, making happy sounds about the gifts, Danielle broke from the kids who'd been watching and came over to me.

"Hello, Chelsea," she said, as if I were her favorite person on earth. "I thought you'd never get here."

"You wish," I said.

Danielle had pulled her sandy curls away from her face with fancy combs. The pale-blue dress she was wearing had a lace collar. Her shoes were copies of the ones I'd abandoned on the kitchen floor. Much as I hated to admit it, she looked great.

"Where's your date?" she asked.

"There." I pointed at Shawn, who was examining the ant farm.

"Gee," said Danielle. "I thought Rachel's little brother had sneaked into the party."

After Rachel's mother and aunt helped Rachel move her gifts onto a chair next to the stairs, Aunt

Ginger turned on the sound system. The overhead light went out and the two women disappeared into the darkness near the stairs.

"Let's dance," said Rachel.

From the depths of the gloom came C.R.'s voice. "I'm hungry," he said. "Why don't we have a couple of sandwiches first?"

Since I'd been too nervous to eat much dinner, I was hungry too. "Which way's the food table?" I asked. "Why is it so dark in here?"

"Take off the sunglasses, stupid," said Danielle.

I'd forgotten I was wearing sunglasses. After I'd parked them on top of my head, I could see better, but I still had no worries about eye damage from exposure to intense light. I headed for the food table.

Rachel's mother and her aunt had put out a good spread. In the middle of a long table sat a very large birthday cake, the most beautiful one I've ever seen. Pale-pink icing was decorated with darker-pink rosebuds, red roses, and green leaves. In the middle of all the rosebuds and roses, Rachel's name was written in dark pink squiggly lines of icing.

Surrounding the cake were dozens of cupcakes, frosted in chocolate and vanilla. Since the cake hadn't been cut and there was no sign of a knife, I ate a cupcake while I decided what to scarf up next.

In addition to cake, the table held four platters of sandwiches and bowls of chips, pretzels, and popcorn. Near the chips was a bowl of dip and cut-up vegetables. I wolfed down a couple of sandwiches, then headed for a can of pop in a tub of ice at one end of the table.

I was no longer hungry, but on the way to the pop I ate another sandwich and handful of chips. I'd selected a can from the tub and was snapping the pull tab when Jerome gave me a friendly punch on the arm.

"Watch it," I warned as the pop splashed. "How are you guys?"

"Terrific." Jerome had a smear of white icing on his chin. He was holding Kendra's hand, which was going to give Danielle something else to talk about.

"Your outfit is pretty," Kendra told me.

"Yours too." Kendra was wearing a black knit top with a red, yellow, and black plaid taffeta skirt. She had a wide black velvet sash around her waist and a matching bow in her hair.

"How do you like the decorations?" she asked.

"Rachel, Danielle, Jill, and I put them up this afternoon."

"Super." I looked around the room. Strands of alternating white and pink crepe-paper streamers were suspended in a circle from the ceiling light in the middle of the room. The streamers fell in long curves, then rose again when they reached the walls, giving the effect of a pink-and-white tent roof. Bunches of balloons were tied in corners, and large silver letters spelled out HAPPY BIRTHDAY across the wall over the food table.

Near the sound system was a cleared area surrounded by chairs. I guessed that area was supposed to be a dance floor. Danielle had managed to drag Ryan onto it, but he was just standing, watching Danielle dance around him. Nearby, Lindsey was talking with Mary Beth and Josh. "Who'd Lindsey bring?" I asked. Lindsey had been very secretive, refusing to tell anybody what boy she'd invited.

"Her brother," said Kendra. "He's over there, playing Nintendo." She pointed at the knot of boys huddled around a video screen on the other side of the dance floor. "Where's your guy, Chelsea?"

"Uh. His name is Shawn. He was here a minute

ago." I looked around, hoping I wouldn't spot Shawn, but he was only five feet away, devouring a sandwich. "There," I said, jerking my head in his direction.

"I know him," Jerome said.

"You do?" I looked back at Shawn, who removed a small piece of lettuce from his sandwich, carefully wiped the mayonnaise off it onto his slacks, and put it into one of his jacket pockets.

"Uh-huh," said Jerome. "He and my little brother played ball in the same league last summer."

"They did?"

Jerome didn't answer. Pulling Kendra with him, he walked over to Shawn. "What's happening, man?" he said.

"Nothing much, man," Shawn told him.

"You going out for ball again this summer?"

"Yeah."

That was when Ryan escaped from the dance floor. He headed for the food table, Danielle chasing after him. She was plenty close enough to hear what the boys said next.

"You'll be facing stiffer competition this summer," Jerome told Shawn, "since you're moving into the fourth-grade league."

"Fourth grade?" echoed Danielle. Then she added, "You're in the *third* grade now?"

"Yeah, but I'm big for my age," said Shawn, as if that was something to be proud of.

I moved closer to him. "My sister told me you're in seventh, Shawn," I said.

"What's this stuff with Shawn?" asked Jerome. "Are you tired of being called Marvin?"

"Marvin?" I said.

Shawn-Marvin ducked his head between his shoulders.

"I don't get it." I grabbed his sandwich, forcing him to look at me. "What *is* your name?" I demanded.

"Ah, most of the time I go by Marvin."

"His older brother's name is Shawn," Jerome told me. "He has a brother in high school too."

"And he's in the third grade." Danielle's voice was filled with joy. "Chelsea's date is a kid in the third grade!"

Twelve

W hy?" I yelled at Marvin. The music had stopped for some reason, and I had everyone's attention. This included Rachel's aunt, who'd come partway down the steps with another bowl of pretzels. "Why are you here instead of Shawn?"

"Shawn couldn't make it, so your sister paid me three dollars and fifty cents to fill in. Can I have my sandwich back?"

I gave Marvin his sandwich.

"A third grader who had to be *paid*," cooed Danielle.

"Oh shut up, Danielle," said C. R.

"I won't. Chelsea's been bragging for weeks about bringing a terrific older boy to the party. Then in reality her date turns out to be him." Danielle pointed at Marvin. "I don't see why I should be the one to shut up."

"Because you're the one with the big mouth."

"Well, I like that!" said Danielle. "I'm only trying to get Chelsea to realize the rest of us aren't stupid enough to fall for her little tricks."

While C.R. and Danielle were arguing, Rachel's aunt put the pretzels on the food table. Then she went to the sound system and put in a new tape. "Rachel has a lot of board games if you kids are interested," she announced, handing a game to Ryan. When she headed back toward the stairs, Ryan put the game on top of a speaker and edged closer to our group.

"Want a bite of my sandwich?" Marvin asked me. "It's pretty good."

"I know," I told him. "I already ate three." I checked out the food again. "Maybe I'll have another cupcake."

"I don't believe her!" said Danielle. "She makes a complete fool of herself and all she can think of is stuffing her stomach."

I hoped C.R. would tell Danielle to shut up again, but he was too busy trying to get away from Rachel, who had a death grip on one of his arms. "Let go," he muttered. He rubbed at his face with his free hand. "What's that smell?"

"Perfume." Rachel shoved a wrist under C.R.'s nose. "Danielle gave it to me. Doesn't it smell good?"

C.R. didn't answer. He was wiggling his nose like a rabbit. Then he wiggled his whole face. He rubbed at his nose, took a deep breath and—"AH-CHOO!" Despite the sneeze, Rachel kept her grip on his arm.

C.R. sneezed three or four more times. "I'm allergic to perfube," he said, and sneezed again.

As I took another cupcake, Rachel finally let go of C.R.'s arm. Danielle and she wandered over to Lindsey's brother, who was kneeling by the tub of pop, taking cans from the ice and building them into a tower. Jerome and Kendra headed for the dance floor.

"My music teacher wants me to audition for the youth symphony," I heard Ryan tell Gina.

"On what?"

"Cello. My mom's not sure she can drive me to rehearsals if I get in."

Gina said something, but I didn't hear what, because the tower of pop cans went over with a crash.

Chad tripped over one of the rolling cans and almost fell, but righted himself, which was a good thing. He was carrying Rachel's ant farm. He brought it over to our group at the food table. "Watch," he told us. "I'm going to drive these ants crazy."

"Shake that ant farm and you're dead meat," said Marvin.

"Oh, yeah?" Chad scowled at Marvin.

"Yeah."

"Says you and who else?"

"My big brothers." Marvin's little smirk came back on his face. It didn't seem as repulsive as it had when I first met him.

Chad must have decided to play safe. He put the ant farm on the table next to the birthday cake and grabbed a handful of chips.

Except for Jerome, who was dancing with Kendra, and the kids playing Nintendo, most of the boys were hanging around the food table. A couple of girls were watching the video players, and some were with Rachel and Lindsey's brother at the tub of pop. Amy, Lanie, and Jill were giggling in a corner near the stairs. My eyes slid past them to the dance floor, and then to the new pop tower going up. I glanced at Marvin. He was putting another piece of lettuce into his pocket.

"Keeping it for later?" I asked him.

"It's for Fredo." Marvin's smirk turned into a real smile.

"Who's Fredo?"

Rachel's aunt Ginger must have turned up the lights when she started the tape, because the room seemed lighter than before. I had no trouble at all seeing what Marvin pulled out of his pocket.

"My frog." He reached both hands into his jacket pocket, then removed them cupped around something. "I caught him this afternoon and thought he might want something refreshing."

"Frogs don't eat lettuce, you nerd," said Chad, who was now holding the chip bowl and eating directly from it.

"The lettuce is to make him feel more at home," Marvin said with great dignity.

"Don't hold him so tight," I said. "Let him breathe."

Rachel and Mary Beth drifted away from the pop tower, approaching to see what we were talking about.

Marvin opened a little space between his thumbs. A tiny creature, almost the same color as peanut butter, poked his head into view. The creature had yellow eyes and looked as if he were wearing a dark-brown mask.

"He's cute," said Mary Beth.

"What's his name?" asked Rachel.

"Fredo," said Marvin.

Danielle, who'd followed Rachel, folded her arms across her chest and looked disgusted.

"There's one in my other pocket too." Marvin twisted so a lumpy jacket pocket swung in my direction. "You can hold him, Chelsea."

I thought the frog would try to escape, but he didn't. I lifted him gently from the pocket, leaving a gap between my thumbs so he could see out.

"That's Redo," said Marvin as the frog peered through the gap.

Rachel admired Redo from a safe distance, but Danielle practically stuck her nose into the frog's air hole.

"Go ahead, Danielle," Ryan said, "kiss him and turn him into a munchkin."

"He's awful pale," said Rachel. "I thought frogs were supposed to be green."

"It was the thought of kissing Danielle," C.R. explained.

I laughed along with the other kids, but I have to admit I felt a tiny bit sorry for Danielle. As she straightened, she blinked rapidly, as if holding back tears.

"He'll get darker to match the other one," said Marvin. "See? His mask is already beginning to show."

The tape was still playing, but Jerome and Kendra had stopped dancing to come look at the frogs. At the sight of Redo, Jerome said, "He looks like he plans to rob a bank."

Redo made a comment, not very loudly. The comment sounded like, "Quack, quack."

"Hey!" Chad said. "He quacked like a duck!"

Kendra stood on tiptoe to see over C. R.'s shoulder.

"In reality—" began Danielle, but Chad interrupted her.

"Listen!"

Danielle made a face but kept quiet.

Redo was silent too. Then a tiny quacking sound came from Marvin's hands.

"I told you!" shouted Chad. "Just like a duck!"

That was when Redo decided to escape. He gave a powerful push against my palm and shot out the crack between my thumbs. He landed on the ant farm and jumped again—right onto the top of the pink birthday cake. He sat there between two rosebuds, looking like part of the decorations.

"There's a frog on my cake," said Rachel.

Redo decided to jump again, but as he pushed off, his back feet sank into the soft icing. He leaned forward onto his front legs, but they sank too. The more poor Redo struggled, the more mired down he became in frosting. He totally destroyed one rosebud and shoved the other one three inches toward the edge of the cake.

"*In* my cake." Rachel sounded stricken.

I rescued the frog, picking him out of the sticky mess and holding him up between two fingers. Redo dangled in midair, his bottom half and arms encased in a suit of pink icing. Crumbs of chocolate cake clung to the long toes of one foot. He looked very depressed.

"I know!" Although he was standing right beside me, Chad was practically shouting. "Let's have frog races!"

"No fair," I protested. "Redo's covered with icing. He can't jump like this."

"Dunk him in water," said Jerome. "He'll be as good as new."

Lindsey's brother dumped the pretzel bowl onto the table and filled it with water from the tub of pop. I dunked Redo until he was clean again. Although the water was very cold, the frog didn't seem to mind at all.

While I was cleaning Redo, the other kids cleared a path from the food table to the tape deck. They set up lanes, marking them with trails of peanuts and pretzels.

Marvin and I knelt at the starting line, our frogs in position.

C.R. held one arm over his head, waiting until the room was completely silent and all eyes were on the challengers. "Ready," he said, then let a couple seconds pass. "Set . . . go!"

Redo took off like a professional racing frog, which meant he jumped in the direction he was supposed to. Fredo jumped straight into the air, landed on Marvin's shoulder, and jumped again. His last jump took him under the food table.

"Everybody stand back!" ordered C.R. "We need light for the search team."

Marvin disappeared from view under the long tablecloth. Chad and Ryan crawled under the tabletop too, and Jerome stuck his head under the cloth.

Redo, captured by me as he reached the finish line, waited patiently in my hands.

There was a sound of a crash from under the table. Somebody—I think Chad—swore. There were scuffling sounds, then a yell: "Get him!"

One of the boys grunted.

"Touch that frog and you're one sad dude," warned Marvin.

Chad backed from beneath the table. One of his heels caught on the cloth and pulled it partway to the floor, dragging a bowl of potato chips with it. Luckily, the bowl was plastic and didn't break, but the chips scattered all over the floor.

Jerome straightened and held up the cloth for the other boys. A few seconds later, Ryan emerged holding Fredo, followed by Marvin.

"Thanks," Marvin said as he accepted the frog from Ryan.

I glanced at Rachel, afraid she might be really upset by the mess. She was watching the action, an expression of stunned fascination on her face. Since she didn't seem ready to make a fuss, I announced, "Redo won the first race."

"That was only practice," said Marvin.

"He won fair and square," I insisted, "but we'll go

two out of three if you want. Redo's one to Fredo's zip."

"All right." Marvin whispered something to Fredo.

"Gentlemen, take your positions." C.R. raised an arm toward the ceiling.

"How do you know Redo's a man?" I asked.

"Just get your frog to the starting line, Chelsea," C.R. said.

"Anyone putting money on Fredo?" asked Chad.

"*Behind* the starting line," Marvin told me.

Redo was a real champion. He'd managed to pull partway out of my hands, his front legs across the starting line and braced for action.

"I bet a quarter on Redo!" shouted Chad. "Come on! Who wants to bet?"

"What on earth is going on here?" came an adult voice.

Rachel's mother and her aunt Ginger were surveying the room from the stairs, Mrs. Porter one step lower than Aunt Ginger. Mrs. Porter's eyes hesitated on Marvin and me, then swept on to the food table.

"Your cake!" she said. "Rachel! What happened to your beautiful birthday cake?"

"I'll put a quarter on Fredo," said Jerome, who

evidently didn't realize that the races had just been canceled.

The women came the rest of the way down the steps and made their way through the crowd to the food table.

"What a mess." Mrs. Porter looked from the mangled birthday cake to the pile of pretzels on the table and the crushed chips on the floor. She pushed a platter of sandwiches back from the edge of the table and tried to straighten the cloth.

"Why is my pretzel bowl full of dirty water?" asked Aunt Ginger.

"We needed it to wash down a frog," Jerome said, very politely.

"In my food bowl?"

"Actually the frogs were quite clean," I explained. "One was just a little bit sticky."

That was when Rachel decided to cry. She moaned a little, gave a sob, and put her hands over her face.

"Oh, honey." Mrs. Porter put her arms around Rachel. "Don't cry. It's only a cake."

"But we were going to save some for when Grandma and Grandpa come tomorrow," said Rachel between sobs, "and chocolate marshmallow cake is my favorite."

"It's all Chelsea's fault," Danielle said. "She invited a little kid to the party and he brought frogs in his pockets."

Mrs. Porter shook her head slightly, sighed, and dropped a kiss on Rachel's forehead. "Your sister's here to pick you up, Chelsea," she told me. "The rest of you kids better start cleaning up in here."

Marvin and I left the party to the sound of applause mixed with a few hisses and boos. My heart sank, but I tried to keep up a brave front. As we passed the end of the food table, I snagged a cupcake that had rolled away during the frog hunt. I peeled and ate it on the way to the car.

"You have a good time?" asked Marty as we climbed into the backseat.

"Great," said Marvin, "best party I ever went to."

"Chelsea?" Juliet sounded very cautious, as if she was afraid I might still be mad at her.

"It was all right." I licked icing off my thumb. "I probably had a better time with Marvin than I would have had with Shawn."

"Thanks," Marvin said. "Want to race frogs tomorrow?"

"You'd better set them free. After Redo's trauma and all the excitement, they deserve a break."

"Okeydokey," Marvin agreed, so cheerfully he aroused my suspicions.

"I mean it," I said.

"You agreed, little brother," added Marty, "and I'm making sure you deliver."

"All right," Marvin said. "Plenty more frogs where they came from."

"Show me." I imagined a place where there were dozens of cute little frogs, sitting under ferns and on top of mossy rocks. "I want to catch my own robber frogs."

When he didn't answer, I added, "Please, Marvin."

"I'll call you sometime," Marvin promised. "We can go frog crawling together."

Thirteen

After the party I wasn't sure how the other kids would act toward me. Although Marvin and I, and most of the kids, had had fun with Fredo and Redo, I suspected that at least Rachel and Danielle were mad at me. One thing was certain: I hadn't proved I was just like the other girls.

"How was the party after we left?" I asked Gina when I called her on Sunday.

"B-o-r-i-n-g. We finished cleaning up. Then Rachel's mother tried to get us to play board games, but no one was interested. Danielle starting picking on Lindsey because Lindsey'd brought her brother to the party. Jill and I worked a picture puzzle, or most of one. A lot of the pieces were missing."

"Sounds like a thrill a minute."

"Yeah." Gina sounded grumpy, so I didn't try to find out anything else about the party. But the rest of the day I worried over Rachel and Danielle. I remembered Rachel's beautiful cake and how Redo had ruined it. I also remembered the boos and hisses among the applause when we'd left the party.

On Monday morning I met Gina at the corner and walked to school with her as usual. At the doorway of Room 14, I hesitated, then followed her inside. I was going to have to face the kids in our class sooner or later.

"Hello, Rachel," I said as I passed her desk.

Rachel looked up from the homework she was finishing. "Hi, Chelsea," she said, sounding like every other morning.

At least Rachel didn't hate me. Encouraged, I said hello to Danielle as I slid into my seat.

Danielle didn't answer.

"I'm sorry if I did something to make you mad at me," I told her.

Danielle turned in her seat to speak to Gina. "Tell the social retard I don't want anything to do with her ever again," she said. "In reality, she's embarrassing."

Blood rushed to my cheeks. For a few terrible seconds I thought I'd burst out crying.

Then Jerome spoke up. "Gee, Chelsea," he said. "How'd you get so lucky?"

"Yeah, Chelsea," said Ryan. "What's your secret formula?"

I was grateful Jerome and Ryan stuck up for me, but inside I was convinced that Danielle was right. Although I'd had a good time Saturday, from Monday morning the party looked like a disaster. All I'd had to do was invite a boy my age, dress up in hose and heels, and act civilized. Instead, I'd taken a third grader, worn my old sandals, gobbled food like I'd never heard of manners, and gotten down on my hands and knees to play with frogs. I had been myself.

And myself wasn't good enough.

While the rest of the class learned about fractions, the constitution, and reproduction, I worried over my future. It was clear that when girls like Jill, Gina, and Rachel were enjoying the high-school prom, I'd be sitting at home watching a video. When I was in college, normal girls would be invited to dances and parties on Saturday nights, leaving me to work in some stinky chemistry lab or alone in my room with the TV. The other girls would eventually have careers and would get married. I'd probably snag cupcakes off the food tables at weddings and baby showers, make stupid comments, and hope for a little kid to ask me to go frog crawling.

The truth was that once again I'd failed to act like the other girls. I'd never, ever be able to fit in anywhere, not here, not at college, not anywhere in my entire life.

After dismissal that afternoon I walked Gina the whole way to her house. My plan was to ask her if there was any possible hope left for me. Instead, I ended up listening to Gina complain about her own life.

"Every single stupid day!" she fumed. She grabbed my arm, forcing me to look at her. Behind her glasses her eyes were resentful. "I'm practically a slave!"

"I thought you liked to practice."

Gina let go of my arm. She walked a few steps, stomping her feet as if she were trying to break the pavement. "Mostly it's not too bad," she admitted, "but sometimes I think I can't bear it another minute. My head aches, and my back aches, and I feel as if I'm going to explode into a million pieces." She shuddered, then wrapped her arms around herself as if she were freezing cold. "Our living room seems to shrink until there's nothing left on earth except me and that giant piano. It stinks of lemon furniture polish, and brass, and old wood. The white keys are like teeth grinning up at me and the black ones remind me of cavities."

Trying to make her feel better, I said, "Playing the piano makes you special."

"I don't want to be special!" Gina yelled. "I'm tired of practicing, and I'm *sick* of being a freak!" Mimicking Mrs. Byler, our school music teacher, she said, "Oh, Gina, you're sooo talented. It's soooo lovely to hear you play. Isn't it *fun* to be sooooo talented?"

"It's better than being a zebra in a herd of ponies," I pointed out.

Gina went still, her eyes losing their angry expression. "A zebra in a herd of ponies?" she said.

"Jill was right. I'm different—like a zebra in a herd of ponies."

Gina started to smile. "Forget Jill," she told me. "Forget Danielle too. They're just jealous."

"Maybe," I muttered.

"For sure." Gina gave me a quick hug. "You're a super friend, and I like you just the way you are."

After I left Gina, I thought about what she'd said and decided she probably didn't understand. Gina's no freak, and she's very talented. Everybody says so. She'll probably have a big career in the music world, and a husband and children too, if that's what she wants.

As for me, I didn't have a choice. Like it or not, I was doomed to be different.

Fourteen

~~~~~~~~~~~~~~

I couldn't forget Danielle, not when I had to deal with her almost every day. She was acting as if I didn't exist.

Gina thought I should take comfort in the fact that Rachel wasn't mad at me. But I was convinced it was only a matter of time until she stopped talking to me also. To make matters worse, weeks passed and Marvin didn't call. I figured he'd forgotten his promise to take me frog crawling. Gina seemed my one true friend, and she was spending more and more hours practicing the piano.

I spent a lot of time on my VIP report, much more than I had on any other assignment. That was because I was beginning to feel sympathy, as well as admiration, for Dian Fossey. She'd done some ugly things to protect the gorillas, things like shooting cattle and destroying food belonging to poachers. Because of this, a lot of people didn't approve of her. Like me, Dian was often depressed and lonely.

Marvin finally called the last week of the month. "It's me," he announced cheerfully when Mom handed me the phone. "Want to go frog crawling Saturday?"

"What took you so long?"

"It's only been a few weeks. You change your mind?"

"No," I said hastily. "What time?"

"About one o'clock. Marty'll give us a ride to the pond, but we'll have to walk home."

"Okay." I could hear noise in the background at Marvin's house. A tape or a radio was playing. Someone was yelling over the sound of it.

"Wait a second," said Marvin. I could hear a muffled conversation, and then he came back on the line. "Bring a backpack and some jars," he told me.

"Why?"

"In case you want to bring anything home. Peanut-butter jars are best." He hesitated, then added, "You can bring a friend too."

"Anything else?" I asked sarcastically. "Pop? Ham sandwiches? Maybe a pizza?"

116

"That's a great idea," he replied. "Catch you later."

Although Gina wanted to go frog crawling with us, she called Saturday morning early to say she couldn't. "Mom is taking me to a big mall near Cleveland to shop for a dress for the concert," she told me. "We'll probably be gone all day."

"Poor you," I sympathized. Personally I'd much rather dig around in a swamp than spend an entire day trying on clothes.

"Poor you too," said Gina. "Did you look outside?"

"No." I didn't have to, since I could hear the steady beat of rain on the roof. I hoped it would stop before Marvin and Marty came to pick me up.

When the phone rang again, I was afraid it was Marvin canceling because of rain. I picked up the receiver, but Juliet had already answered upstairs.

"Hello," she said in a sleepy voice.

In a way I was glad that Juliet answered the phone first. When I heard Dad's voice, I got a terrible surge of homesickness, which was really stupid because I was already home. I stood listening to him and Juliet talk, holding back tears and wishing my stomach would stop lurching around. Luckily, by the time he got around to asking for me, I had everything under control.

"Don't forget you're coming to D.C. over spring break," Dad told us right before saying good-bye. "I hope the cherry trees are still in bloom."

"Me too," I said.

"I'll be the tall guy in the blue suit," he added.

Both Juliet and I laughed out loud. How could Dad think we'd forget how he looks?

Although the rain had stopped by the time Marty pulled up in front of our house that afternoon, a thick gray layer of clouds seemed to hang a few feet above the treetops. I gathered my gear, including a rain jacket, and trudged out to the car.

"Where's the food?" asked Marvin.

"In my stomach," I told him.

When I crawled into the backseat, another kid was sitting there—a kid who looked very familiar.

"Who are you?" I demanded, as if I didn't already know he was Shawn, the almost-eighth-grader who'd refused to be seen at Rachel's party with me.

"Shawn," he said.

"Oh." I tried to sound as much like Danielle as possible. "Him."

"Yep." Shawn had the same smirk as Marvin, not at all like the wide smile of his picture.

"What happened to your hair?" There was no sign of black curls beneath the red baseball cap he was wearing.

"I had it cut off."

"I thought maybe you were exposed to nuclear fallout."

"Thanks. I like your looks too."

That was our total conversation in the car. We sat like two robots, staring at the backs of Marvin's and Marty's heads. I don't know what Shawn was thinking, but I figured he was getting off easy. I'd hurt his feelings for a couple of minutes, but he'd ruined my entire future.

A short distance from town, Marty turned into a dirt lane marked by a large sign. The sign read:

KEEP OUT!

NO TRESPASSING!

THIS MEANS YOU!

Marty drove down the lane and stopped in a weedy clearing near an abandoned house.

The house sagged to the left as if it had been hit by

a high wind. The front porch sagged the opposite direction, and the front door hung partway off its hinges. Most of the windows were broken or missing. A faded red curtain waved like a tattered flag from an empty frame on the second floor. Signs were nailed to the first-floor walls and porch. KEEP OUT! warned most of them. The others made threats about what would happen to people who trespassed.

"Are we allowed here?" I asked Shawn as we unloaded the trunk of the car.

"Yeah." He was buckling a heavy leather belt around his waist. The belt had slots that held a knife, a pair of scissors, and what looked like giant tweezers. He slung a backpack over his shoulders, glanced at Marvin, who was weighed down by similar equipment, and then picked up a couple of things that resembled butterfly nets.

"Grab that stuff, will you?" He jerked his head toward a yellow bucket and a large long-handled sieve, the only items left in the trunk besides the spare tire.

I took the sieve and bucket, then slammed the trunk lid shut. "How can I be sure we aren't trespassing?" I said as I watched the car move away from us and into a turn.

Instead of answering me, Shawn held out one of the nets. "Carry this," he said.

"Listen, Mr. Big-Deal Shawn Davis!" I dropped the sieve and bucket on the ground, put my fists on my hips, and glared at him. "Marvin invited *me* to hunt frogs with *him*. I didn't agree to break any laws, and I sure didn't agree to be a pack animal for a stuck-on-himself sexist nerd."

"Wow," said Marvin.

After Shawn stared at me a couple of seconds, his smirk widened into a grin. "This property belongs to my uncle in Florida," he explained, "and he likes my family to keep an eye on it. I'm doing a science project out here during the spring and summer."

By that time Marty and his car were almost to the main road. Still angry, I ignored the net Shawn held toward me, but picked up the sieve and the bucket. I fell in behind the boys as they headed toward the trees on the other side of the abandoned house.

"You expect me to believe you'll be working on a school project during the summer?" I asked Shawn's back.

He grunted, which was the only answer I received until we descended a rough trail through weeds and woods to a clearing. When Marvin and Shawn halted at the edge of the clearing, I pushed between them to see the pond.

Where we were standing, soggy ground blended into moss-covered banks and stretches of mud. To the right, the bank dropped out of sight into a dip in the earth. From the sound of water running and a slight movement in the surface of that part of the pond, I guessed a stream had made the dip.

"Mr. Rutledge, the biology teacher at the high school, is gathering information on mudpuppies in this area," Shawn explained. "I'm keeping track of other pond animals."

When I didn't say anything, he said, "It's part of the enriched program."

I took a deep breath, trying to sample the air the way a cat does. It smelled of fresh rain, moss, and dead fish. I took another breath and detected wet leaves, mushrooms, and mud.

Overhead, the clouds had turned pale gray. In the silvery light, the moss was a deep, moist green, and the mud flat near the edge of the pond had a slick, almost oily surface. The trees we were standing under were black where their branches and trunks were wet.

"The ground's still pretty soggy," Shawn observed as he stepped into the clearing. When he shifted his weight from one foot to the other, the moss made a sucking sound.

"I don't care," I told him. "These are old sneakers. I can even wear them into the water if I want to."

"I'm going to poke around in the woods," Marvin said, "try to catch a couple of robber frogs."

"Wood frogs," corrected Shawn. "Don't forget to write down where you find them." He glanced at me. "I don't suppose you brought a note pad."

"Nobody told me I was taking part in an important science project." I moved away from him, skirting the stretch of mud, and headed toward the dip where the bank overhung the water.

"Where are you going?" asked Shawn.

"Over there." I pointed toward the overhang. "If I lie on my belly, I might see something in the water under the bank."

"Want a net?"

"If you don't need it."

"I can't use two at once." As he handed me the net, Shawn asked, "Will you fill a jar with pond water from over there? I like to keep a check on what's in it."

"Okeydokey," I agreed.

I found a spot where the current from the stream

wasn't strong enough to stir the muddy bottom, and lay on my stomach. Because of the movement of water from the stream, or maybe because the temperature wasn't warm enough, there wasn't much algae. It was too early in the spring for duckweed to cover the surface, so I could see a distance into the water.

By July the pond would be filled with duckweed and algae. All kinds of water bugs, insects, water plants, and fish would make it their home. There might even be lily pads on its surface, new cattails, and ferns growing on and near the mossy banks. Lying motionless, I waited for life in the water the way Dian Fossey had waited for gorillas in the jungle and mud of a mountain rain forest.

I rested my chin on my hands. The moss beneath my fingers was wet, the ground soft and spongy under my body. School, the other kids, and my problem with fitting in still existed, but I had escaped into a different world. Like Dian, I'd found a magic place—only my place was close to home, beneath me in the pond.

Fifteen

~~~~~~~~~~

A school of minnows passed, returned, and disappeared in seconds. An empty snail's shell, smaller than the tip of my little finger, was tugged gently back and forth by the current. Directly below my face was a flat stone covered by silt, its shape practically invisible against the muddy bottom.

There was a flick of tail, and a narrow bright fish was almost gone before I'd seen it. Unaware of me, another appeared at the edge of my vision. The fish's back was slate blue. Its lower sides and stomach flashed golden yellow as the bluegill twisted, then swam deeper, out of sight.

A puff of mud, like smoke, jetted from under the rock. Careful so that no movement would reflect in the water, I eased a hand from beneath my chin and shoved the sleeve of my jacket above the elbow. As mud puffed again, I froze. A small reddish claw appeared from the lower edge of the rock.

I realized I was holding my breath and exhaled steadily, then slipped my hand smoothly, without a ripple, into the pond and downward until my fingers hovered above the rock.

The water was so cold, the bones ached inside my arm to my elbow, then to my shoulder. Moisture soaked through my jacket, and the legs of my jeans were wet. I bit my lower lip and tried to keep from shivering.

The white skin of my arm looked dead through the water, but when I wiggled my fingers, they came alive, reminding me of a pale octopus, lurking out of sight of the crayfish beneath the rock.

Another tiny claw appeared, then antennae, and finally the small body, like a miniature lobster.

I pounced. The crayfish was mine. I admired him for a few seconds, then put him in a peanut-butter jar filled with pond water.

"Chelsea!"

My name was half whispered, half shouted. Shawn motioned me toward him.

I put the jar with the crayfish and the rest of my

gear on the bank beside Shawn's stuff, before wading into the water to join him.

"Help me move this." Shawn leaned over a partly submerged log, grasping the small end of it in one hand, the other holding his large net.

The log had been under water so long that the first piece I grabbed came away in my hands. What was left looked rotten too, so I bent over, shoved my arms into the water to my shoulders, and laced my fingers beneath it. I braced my feet in the slippery mud of the pond bottom.

The log was a lot heavier than I'd expected. For a couple of seconds, I didn't think I could lift it, but I gritted my teeth and forced my arms upward. Up and over . . .

"Don't drop it!" Shawn yelled.

Something long, dark, and snaky streaked through the water.

I screeched, but hung on to my end of the log.

"Gotcha!" Shawn scooped his net through the pond and out again. He waded ankle-deep through mud to the bank where he dumped his captive into a yellow bucket. "Hey, hey," he said.

"What is it?"

Ignoring my question, Shawn ordered, "Get water." He leaned over, hands on his knees, staring into the bucket.

I ran to bring water. "Who was your slave last week?" I demanded as I poured.

"Marvin." Shawn grinned at me. His red cap lay on the bank near my crayfish jar. The hair on top of his head was longer than on the sides and back, long enough to form black curls.

"What is it?" I asked a second time. The creature in the bucket was tube shaped and dark brown. Except for short legs protruding from its body, it looked a lot like a snake.

"A mudpuppy."

"Sure is ugly." I bent to examine the mudpuppy more closely. "What are those red things on its neck?" I pointed at two fernlike growths.

"Gills."

"On the outside of its body?"

"Right." Shawn leaned over the bucket too, his head close to mine. "This is the first mudpuppy I've ever caught," he said.

Personally, I preferred my crayfish. "I saw a school of minnows and a couple of other fish," I told him.

"One was a bluegill, but I didn't get a good look at the other one."

Shawn made a noise, which I guessed was his answer.

"I caught a crayfish," I said.

While Shawn was looking at my crayfish, Marvin emerged from the trees. He'd captured a single wood frog, which was hunched on the bottom of a jar, looking pale and miserable. "There were two," Marvin told us, "but one of them got away."

"We'd better head back to town," said Shawn as Marvin admired Shawn's catch. "I don't want to keep the mudpuppy in the bucket any longer than I have to. There might not be enough oxygen in the water."

"What will you do with him?" I began to gather up my gear, stowing the jar with the crayfish in my backpack.

"Give him to Mr. Rutledge."

Since Shawn had to take extra care of the bucket, Marvin and I carried most of the other gear. We went in single file back through the trees and down the weedy trail, past the house until we came to the lane, where we were able to walk side by side. On the way I thought about watching the fish and catching the crayfish. I felt kind of strange, as if I'd taken off a heavy coat or were floating, instead of trudging down a muddy lane. I felt light inside too.

At first I thought all this lightness was the sign of an empty stomach. But by the time we reached the main road, I'd discovered what really caused it.

I *was* hungry, and cold and wet. My sneakers and jeans were slimy with mud, and I needed a tissue. But I also was happier than I'd been in a long time — since the day Rachel had given out the party invitations, the day Danielle accused me of being socially retarded.

"How did you get to work on this project?" I asked Shawn.

"I helped a high-school kid with his science experiment when I was in the sixth grade," he said. "Last summer Mr. Rutledge invited me to take part in a biology project studying pond life. He needed volunteers for the mudpuppy project this summer and he picked me."

"Lucky." My voice was filled with jealousy, but I didn't care. I *was* jealous.

"You want to help?" Shawn glanced at me as we reached city sidewalks. "We could use another kid."

"Sure!" I skipped several steps, heard water slosh

in my crayfish jar, and waited for the boys to catch up. "Thanks! That will be great!"

"You'll have to work every Saturday afternoon until school's out, and two afternoons a week in the summer," he warned. "And every animal taken from the pond has to be returned."

"That's all right with me. I *love* ponds!"

"I told you she'd like slimy stuff," said Marvin.

That was when I noticed two boys on the bridge over the abandoned tracks, not far from Rachel's house. The boys were leaning against the railing, staring down at the tracks, as if they expected a train any minute. When they heard us approach, they looked up.

The boys were C. R. and Ryan.

I glanced down at the slime drying on my jeans and the clumps of mud stuck to my sneakers. Later, when I looked in a mirror, I discovered more mud on my forehead. My hair was a tangled mess, and my nose was running.

Fortunately, I am not boy crazy like Rachel. I walked right up to them and said, "Does either of you have a tissue?"

Ryan had a whole wad of tissues. He fished a clean one out of the wad and gave it to me.

While I was blowing my nose and Ryan and C.R. were looking at the mudpuppy, Marvin said, "I know you guys. You were at that neato party."

"Yeah," said Ryan. "You're the kid who brought the frogs."

"So that's what happened to my wood frogs!" Shawn said.

"Hey, man," said Marvin, "I caught one of them."

Shawn made a sound of disgust. "You owe me the frog in your backpack, little brother," he said, "and you'd better not forget it."

"Want some help carrying stuff?" offered C.R. when I shoved the used tissue in my pocket and began picking up the nets, sieve, and other equipment.

"Just as far as my house," I told him. "Mom will give the guys a ride the rest of the way home."

We set off again, walking faster with the load divided among five people. All I had to carry was my backpack and my crayfish. It only took ten minutes to reach Rachel's house from the railroad bridge.

Rachel and Danielle were sitting on the front steps, painting their fingernails a bloody red. They didn't look up until we were very close.

Shawn, C.R., and I were walking together, with me in the middle. Ryan and Marvin were trailing behind. "I figure it takes a special talent," Marvin was telling Ryan when the other girls noticed us. "If you don't have the talent, forget frogs. Go for something easy to catch, like turtles."

I was a muddy mess and smelled of pond water. Once again, I realized, I was going to look like a fool to Danielle. She probably felt embarrassed for me.

I don't care, I told myself fiercely. I just don't care!

Suddenly, much to my surprise, I discovered that was true. I really *didn't* care if Danielle didn't approve of me. "Hi, Rachel!" I called out. "Hi, Danielle!"

Then the boys and I had passed. I glanced over my shoulder.

Danielle was staring after us, her mouth hanging open and her blue eyes bugged out. Rachel looked as if she were playing statue; one hand held the nail-polish brush in the air, the other clutched a tiny bottle. She recovered fast enough to smile and wave before I turned away. I waved back, then happily headed on home with a crayfish, a mudpuppy, a wood frog—and four boys.

Sixteen

~~~~~~~~~

That evening I tried to write a poem about watching the animals in the pond water, but I couldn't find the right words. Instead, this is what came out:

IN REALITY

*In reality I don't like nail polish
Or shoes that pinch, or having to keep clean
All the time.*

*In reality I like boys—
Maybe better than frogs
But I'm not sure yet.*

*In reality I'm embarrassing
Even to myself sometimes.
But I'm me—
Like nobody else.*

I Was a Fifth-Grade Zebra

The next time Danielle says that in reality I'm socially retarded, I'll just think of my poem and smile mysteriously. I put it in my desk drawer, then checked my VIP report to make certain I didn't leave out the page of notes and the bibliography Mr. Feeny wanted.

Before starting work on my math assignment, I flipped through a book I'd borrowed from the library to help with my research. I stopped at my favorite picture of Dian Fossey—the one where she's holding a baby gorilla she rescued from poachers.

A lot of people didn't like her at all, and one person hated her enough to murder her. But Dian Fossey was a Very Important Person. She left the world a better place because she lived. I stared at her picture and felt happy, the way I'd felt when I was lying on my stomach looking into the water, the way I'd felt walking home with the crayfish.

Dian Fossey was not like everybody else. Without her, there would be no more mountain gorillas living free. She cared more about doing what she knew was right than she cared about being like other people.

I slowly ran a finger over the picture of Dian, as if by touching it I was touching her. Then I thought of Gina and her piano and of Shawn and his pond.

Maybe if I looked closely at the herd of ponies, there would be more zebras mixed among them than I'd ever suspected. It's just that some zebras' stripes are not as noticeable as others'.

And maybe . . . no, not maybe. I was certain of it.

In a herd of ponies, the ones with the stripes—the zebras—are the lucky ones. Lucky Dian. Lucky Gina. Lucky me.

Nancy J. Hopper

is the author of many novels for young people, including *The Queen of Put-Down; The Truth or Dare Trap;* and *The Seven ½ Sins of Stacey Kendall.* A Friday volunteer in a fifth-grade class, she says, "Kids this age are confronted with a combination of the familiar—like math and peer pressure—and the unfamiliar—like changing relationships between boys and girls. For a fifth-grader, fitting in with others is of prime importance, but so is keeping a piece of yourself—to be the person you really are."

Mrs. Hopper lives in Alliance, Ohio, with her husband. They have two children.